Pirate Diary

*W*hen his ship is captured by pirates, nine-year-old cabin boy Jake Carpenter finds himself embarking on an exciting new life on the wrong side of the law! Starting in 1716, *Pirate Diary* describes Jake's adventures as he discovers the thrills and perils of life at sea.

"Like a rollicking adventure but packed with accurate historical detail." *The Financial Times*

"Stands out for the thoughtfulness of the way it is put together, and for its gorgeousness and vitality." *Sunday Times Children's Book of the Week*

Winner of the *Smarties Book Prize Silver Award* and the *Kate Greenaway Medal*

For Jacob
R.P.

For Jack
C.R.

First published 2001 by Walker Books Ltd
87 Vauxhall Walk, London SE11 5HJ

This edition published for Ottakar's 2005

2 4 6 8 10 9 7 5 3 1

Map used on the cover and pages 1, 95, 115 © National Maritime Museum, London

This book has been typeset in Truesdell, Humana Script and La Figura

Printed and bound in Great Britain by Creative Print and Design (Wales), Ebbw Vale

British Library Cataloguing in Publication Data:
a catalogue record for this book
is available from the British Library

ISBN 0-7445-7025-5

www.walkerbooks.co.uk

Pirate Diary

THE JOURNAL OF
Jake Carpenter

RICHARD PLATT
illustrated by CHRIS RIDDELL

OTTAKAR'S

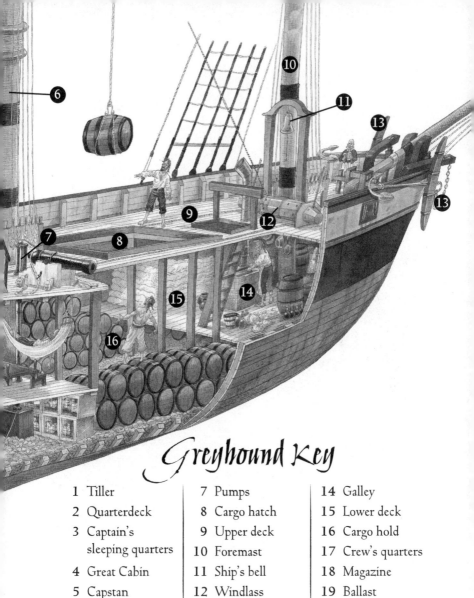

Greyhound Key

THIS IS THE JOURNAL OF

Jake Carpenter

I begin on the twenty-third day of
September in the year 1716. It is the third
year of the reign of our good King George,
and the tenth of my life.

FOR AS LONG as I can remember, I have lived in the
village of Holyoak, North Carolina. My family came to
the American colonies from England. I knew not my
mother, for she died when I was yet a baby. My father,
a medical doctor, raised me with the help of his two
sisters. From them I learned my letters. This was my
only schooling.

Now, though, my life is to change, for I am to GO
TO SEA! My father wants me to study medicine but

believes I should see more of the world first. Thus I am to become a SAILOR – at least for a while.

His plan is that I should join his brother, Will, who is already a seaman. My father sent a letter to the owner of Will's ship, who agreed to take me on the crew.

Now the ship has docked and Will has come to fetch me. He is a fine man. He has the same face as my father, but his hands are larger and rough to the touch. Whenever he is ashore he comes to see us, bringing strange gifts and wondrous yarns. My aunts laugh and call them "when-I-was" tales, for this is how they always begin.

Will has told me of sea monsters, mermaids, and of floating islands made of ice. He has seen a whirlpool, sailed through a hurricane and escaped from pirates. And soon I am to see all of these things FOR MYSELF.

I write this on my last day at home, for tomorrow I shall return with my Uncle Will to his ship, the *Sally Anne*.

Monday 24th

This morn Will woke me before sun-up. He bid me fetch my belongings, but laughed out loud when I did. "Fie, man!" he snorted. "Do you think we are going to sea in a tailor's shop?" With this he emptied half the clothes from my bag. Seeing my glum face, he told me they were the clothes of a landsman. (This, he explained, is what sailors call those who are used to a life ashore.) "Such finery is no use on a ship, and there's precious little space aboard to stow 'em."

Thus lightly loaded we set off at dawn. My father clapped me upon the shoulder, wished me luck and bid Will take care of me. My aunts both hugged me and dabbed my eyes with their aprons (though they would have better dabbed their own, which needed it more).

The journey to Charleston took us all the day and I most eagerly desired to see the sea. When we arrived I said to Will that I had expected the ocean to be bigger, for I thought I spied the other shore in the distance.

"Nay, Jake!" he laughed in reply. "This here is but a wide river. The open ocean is three leagues east and is far too big to see across."

Our inn for the night is a mean and grimy place. Even the straw mattresses are lumpy and dusty.

Tuesday 25th

Today we had some ill luck when we went to join our ship. We were yet two streets away from the quayside when Will stopped suddenly. He gazed up at the masts that towered above the houses. "She's not there," he gasped, pointing upwards. "The *Sally Anne*! Her masthead is gone!" With this he dropped his bag and, forgetting me, raced to the waterside.

When I caught up with him, he was sitting gloomily with the harbour master. He told Will his ship had found a cargo sooner than expected and had sailed on the evening tide. I was sorely disappointed. Forcing a smile, Will said, "Never mind, Jake. Our luck will change."

Then the harbour master added, "*Greyhound* is looking for fit and able men. You could do worse than sign on at yonder inn" – pointing out an ale house – "if you can put up with old Captain Nick!" Will shrugged. "Beggars cannot be choosers."

We found a man from the *Greyhound* sitting in a back room. To my surprise, he asked us no questions, but bid us write our names in a book below the names of other members of the crew. Thus it was that by signing my name I ceased to be just the son of a doctor and became a sailor!

We go aboard tomorrow.

Wednesday 26th

This morning Will and I joined our ship. I felt a true landsman, for in walking up the plank from the quayside I lost my footing. Before I could topple into the water, though, Will hauled me on board. One member of the crew saw my misfortune and, when he had recovered from his laughter, led Will and me down into the ship.

Will took down a roll of canvas and, using the ropes at each end, hung it up between two deck timbers. "This hammock is where you shall sleep, Jake. By day you stow it away with your clothes rolled inside." I was thrice tipped out of my hammock before I learned how to climb into it. Now I am here, though, I find it as comfortable as any bed.

The *Greyhound* is an odd place. I am to live in a world of wood and water. Almost everything I look upon is wood. That which is not wood is canvas, rope or tar.

I was eager to explore the ship, but before I could do this Will set me to wash the decks. He explained that they must be kept damp, or the boards shrink apart, letting in the sea. This was a long and tiresome chore, but when it was complete I was free to watch the seamen load the cargo.

They did this with the aid of one of the ship's yards (these being the stout beams crossing the mast, from which the sails hang). Using ropes fixed to yards, it was easier work to hoist the tubs and barrels from the quayside.

There are two tall masts. The front one, which I must learn to call the foremast, has yards for three great square sails. The mainmast behind it likewise has three of these square sails. But behind this mainmast there is also an odd-shaped sail stretched between two spars, making the shape a little like a letter K. I learned that our ship is called a "brig" on account of this rigging (which is what sailors call the arrangement of the sails, masts and ropes).

Here I must end, for daylight fades. Candles are permitted only inside a horn lantern, which protects the ship against fire. But it also makes the candle's light into a dull glow that is useless for writing.

Thursday 27th

I already have a friend – the cook's boy, Abraham. He promised me, "I'll make sure your belly is never empty if you learn me my letters." This seemed a good deal to me, but after my first meal yesterday my mind was changed. I had food aplenty, but I could not guess what it was, and ate little of it.

The upper deck of the *Greyhound* I measured today by walking: it is thirty of my paces. At the back is the captain's Great Cabin. At least, I am told it is his cabin, but he has yet to come out of it.

Near the back, beneath the upper deck, is a cabin for the rest of us. This is where we sling our hammocks at night and eat our meals by day, at a table let down on ropes.

The hold in the belly of the ship holds the cargo. I am

not allowed to go down there until we are at sea, but from its stink, I guess that we are carrying salted fish. When I ask what is in the hold and where we are bound, Will tells me: "Best not to ask too many questions on board this ship, lad, if you know what is good for you."

My head reels with all I have learned. Every part of the ship has its own strange name. The front is not "front", but "fore" or "stem" or "bows". The back is "aft" or "abaft", or "stern", or "astern". Right is "starboard" and left is "port" (yet some call it "larboard", perhaps just to baffle me further!).

Saturday 29th

In the middle of last night a crewman (it was too dark to see who) pitched me rudely out of my hammock. "Come on, lad, we're getting under way." Still half asleep, I clambered up the companionway (which is a ship's staircase, as steep as a ladder) and on to the deck.

The moon was almost full, and looking around

I could see that my ship-
mates were readying the
Greyhound to leave. It was
then I saw the captain for
the first time. I guessed
who he was, for as soon
as he hissed "Away
aloft" in a low voice
the sailors hurried up
the rigging as if the
devil himself had given
the order.

When the
captain glowered at me, I felt a sudden chill, but before he
could speak to me, Will beckoned me over. "Jake, jump
ashore and loosen the forward rope from yonder bollard.
Let it slide into the water – no splash, now – then run aft
and jump aboard." It took all my strength to unwind the
great rope from the wooden stump on the quayside. The

wind pulled the *Greyhound*'s head away from the dock, and I saw why Will had told me to run aft. A yard of water already separated ship from shore and I had to leap to cross the quickly widening gap.

Above us, sailors unfurled the foresail, and it filled with wind. This was enough to make the *Greyhound* glide smoothly away from the dock and into the channel. The tide had just turned, and the current helped us along. Soon we left the harbour lights of Charleston behind us, and as the sun rose over Sullivan's Island we sailed into the open ocean.

Sunday 30th

I discovered this morning why we sailed at night. Captain Nick owes money to Charleston merchants who stocked the ship, and to craftsmen who repaired it. They would have seized the *Greyhound* if we had not slipped away on the tide. He says that when he returns from this trip, he will pay what he owes with interest. However, I doubt the truth of this, for Will has found out that our captain owes the crew three months' wages. "He will keep back ours too," he told me, "to make sure that we stay with the ship."

Abraham at last answered my questions about the cargo. Apart from the fish, all of it is contraband, which is to say, smuggled goods. Smuggling seems hardly a crime to me. It just means avoiding the customs taxes that ships pay to unload their cargo. Abe says that "Even the king's men who search the ship ignore contraband as long as we give 'em a share!" A couple of our shipmates were listening to us talking and one butted in thus:

"Why should we Americans pay taxes to an English king who cares nothing about us and gives us no say in the way our affairs are run? So we avoid ports in England or Jamaica where we must pay the customs fees. Instead we unload cargoes in Spanish, Dutch and French ports in the West Indies and pay nothing."

Our destination is Martinique, where we shall sell the cargo. As I suspected, we are carrying salt fish, but also rice and timber. We will return with sugar, molasses, Dutch gin, French brandy and lace – all contraband.

OCTOBER
Monday 1st

Until today, Will had been looking after me and setting me chores. But as a jest on my family name, the captain has given me as a servant to Adam, the carpenter. I am to help Adam and learn his work. Already he has taught me the names of all his tools so that I can hand them to him when he needs them.

Tuesday 2nd

Now we are well out to sea the winds and waves are much bigger. Every rope and sail on the *Greyhound* appears stretched to bursting point. Every timber seems to creak and complain, and the seawater licks the deck.

I am very seasick, and suspect that the change of food may not help my guts. We eat mostly a dull stew of beans, with some salt meat and fish and some cheese. The cook told me: "You'd better get to like beans and salty hog, lad. It may be dull but 'tis nutriment enough – and to be sure you shall eat precious little else while we sail." The cook prepares the food with Abraham in a cabin at the bow of the ship. His hearth there is enclosed in bricks to keep the heat from the ship's timbers.

Ship's biscuits (which everyone calls bread) are as hard as nails. When I first bit into my biscuit, I discovered a dozen little white worms that had made tunnels into it. Abraham helped me. "Eat them in the dark. Or if you cannot wait until nightfall, tap them on the deck. This knocks the worms from their homes."

Wednesday 3rd

Adam sent me to climb to the very top of the mainmast, for as well as helping him I must share in the work of sailing the ship. Abraham came with me as my guide.

Though I have climbed many trees, none was like this. Even in a gentle breeze a mast pitches and sways as if it is trying to shake you off. This made me feel sick with fear, but I tried to hide it lest Abraham guessed my alarm.

Abraham and I have the job of setting and handing the upper topsails (which means letting them down and rolling them up). These are the highest and smallest sails, but they are heavy enough. As we grow stronger we shall move down the mast and set the bigger sails. Abraham tried to teach me the names of each of the ten sails. In return I taught him the names of the twenty-six letters. He learned his lesson quicker than I learned mine.

Sunday 7th

Since we left port a powerful ocean current has slowed our progress. Noah, our first mate (he commands us when the captain is ill or sleeping), says, "It is like sailing a ship uphill!" Nor has the wind been kind to us. It seemed unsure which way to blow.

At last though we have sailed into easier waters. The ocean is calmer, and much bluer than it has been until now. The winds are steadier too. This gives us a welcome rest: when the winds change often we must adjust the sails each minute.

This afternoon, Abraham beckoned to me, hissing, "Jake! Come! The captain sleeps in his bunk and I have sneaked out from the Great Cabin a chart, but make haste, for I must replace it before he wakes." On this sea-map he showed me our course and bid me read out the names of places we shall pass by.

Monday 8th

Today Adam showed me measuring and marking when we cut out a rotting deck plank and fitted a new one. "Any fool can cut along a line with a saw," he told me. "The clever part is knowing where to draw the line."

Daniel, the second mate, has a goat for milking (which he shares with none but the captain). Today the goat jumped up on a cannon and ate our day's bread.

Tuesday 9th

The change in the weather and our steady progress have not improved the temper of our captain. This afternoon he spoke only to curse the ship, or d--n the crew, or swear at the wind for not blowing harder.

The only man the captain will listen to is Noah. As first mate, he takes orders from the captain. In truth, Noah manages the ship – and the captain too. He is a skilful navigator. This is to say that he can judge how far the ship has come, and how to steer us onward. All this he tells the captain in his cabin, plotting our course on the chart. When their meeting is over, the captain appears and tells the helmsman in which direction to steer – as if it is he, not Noah, who decides the course.

Wednesday 10th

When Abraham saw me struggling to relieve myself over the deck rail in a strong breeze, he laughed at first, but then grabbed me in alarm, saying, "You will soon be overboard doing that." Then he took me to the ship's waist and showed me the "piss-dale". This is a lead trough that drains into the sea; those using it run no risk of being swept overboard, even in the foulest weather.

Thursday 11th

Saw a man flogged. Captain Nick had been drinking rum until late last night. When he rose, the first man he spied was a seaman working the pumps. (These drain from the hold any water that has leaked in.) The captain judged that he was pumping too slow, and ordered him flogged at sundown.

The poor man's hands were tied above his head to the rail of the quarterdeck. The crew drew cards from a pack to see who would whip him. As luck would have it, one of his friends pulled the lowest card. I guessed he would thus receive a lighter whipping, and at first he did. But seeing that the man held back the whip, the captain ordered him to "Put some effort into it!" Knowing he risked the same punishment if he disobeyed, the poor seaman was forced to whip until his friend's blood sprayed upon the deck. I turned away, but saw those behind me flinch each time the whip came down.

Sunday 14th

This day Noah let me see how he navigates the ship. "To get where we want to go, we must know in which direction we sail; and to know where we are, we must know our speed. Direction is easy," he told me, pointing to the compass. "Its swinging needle is magnetic, lad. The earth is like a giant magnet which attracts the needle. The red end always points north, so we can see instantly our bearing, which is where we are headed."

Noah next explained how to measure how fast the *Greyhound* sails. "We heave into the sea a wooden board on a measuring rope. It is marked with knots every forty-eight feet." Noah showed me how to do it. As the floating cord pulled out the rope from a coil I held, I counted how many knots slipped through my hands before sand in a watchglass ran out. I counted four knots, so our ship shall cover four sea miles each hour, or ninety-six in a day. Noah then rules on the chart a line which shows our day's sailing. Its beginning is our position yesterday; its angle is our bearing; its length is the distance we've sailed; and its end is where we are now.

To check his sums, Noah finds our latitude: how far we have travelled north or south. He does this at noon by measuring the sun's height with a machine called a backstaff. "I stare at the horizon through slits at each end," he told me, "then move the block on the smaller arch until its shadow falls upon the slit at the far end." To get the sun's height Noah reads off numbers alongside each slit and adds them. Looking up the total in an almanac – a book of navigator's tables – gives our latitude.

Thursday 18th

I do not want to write of today's evil acts, for they pain me so much. Yet I must, for I mean this journal to be a true and complete record of my voyage.

This morning, while mopping the deck, I lost a bucket overboard. The captain saw this happen and flew into a rage. At first I could not understand why he valued the bucket so highly, but this evening I learned that sailors believe losing one brings bad luck. For me it has proved unlucky indeed.

The captain yelled to the second mate: "Daniel! Flog the stupidity from that idiot landsman or so help me I'll throw him in the ocean!" The second mate dragged me to a cannon and tied me face down across it.

The crew call him "Do-little-Daniel", for he is the captain's favourite and the only one who dares be seen idle. However, at this task he was most energetic.

I shut my eyes, clenched my teeth and waited for the rope. But then, suddenly, I heard Will cry: "Stop! Spare the lad, Dan, for God's sake; you'll kill him with that rope!"

For a moment there was nothing but the slap of sail and the lapping of waves. Then the captain's voice. A growl at first, it rose and grew into a terrifying roar. "Do you challenge me, man? Who is the captain here? If this boy is not to pay for his stupidity, then YOU shall – and doubly so."

I was glad I could not see what happened next. I wish I had not heard it, either. My uncle's groans as the rope skinned his back sickened me. After I had counted nineteen lashes he fell senseless. Will's tormentors then bundled him into the skiff, the smallest of our three boats – I heard the splash as it was lowered. By the time I was untied, my uncle was hardly more than a dot far astern. He will surely die without any provisions, and it is all because of my awful clumsiness.

The captain's fury is spent, and my punishment has been reduced from flogging to mastheading. Tomorrow I will be sent aloft and must remain there until summoned.

Friday 19th

Soon after dawn I climbed to the foremast top. I was allowed only some water in a leather bottle to quench my thirst. I was fortunate, for the sea was calm and the sun not strong enough to blister my skin. In fact, my "punishment" was more of a rest than a hardship.

When the morning was half gone, a topman climbed to my perch to reef, or roll up, a sail. He brought from his pocket a hard-boiled egg and said, "Here, Jake, I was cleaning out the chicken coop, and I don't see why Captain Nick should have them all." Later, I got a lump of sugar and an apple (which is a rare treasure on a ship) as other topmen took pity on me.

In the afternoon I thought I glimpsed Will on the

horizon waving from his little boat – though perhaps my mind played tricks on me, for by then he would have been far out of sight.

Just before sundown, I really did see another vessel, though the ocean swell often hid it behind the wave-tops. As a reward for my sharp eyes I was allowed to come down and was given a bowl of warming soup.

Saturday 20th

With clubs we all hunted rats in the hold, for they eat the cargo, and there was much betting on who would catch the most. The winner caught nineteen. The lookout saw the ship I first spotted yesterday. She seems to be sailing a similar course to us.

Sunday 21st

Our whole world is turned topsy-turvy! At sunrise this morning the ship was closer and steered towards us. It was flying the Dutch flag. When we came within hailing distance a sailor shouted to us that they needed water. Our captain grudgingly agreed to give them a barrel, for we had plenty, and we shortened sail, slowing the *Greyhound* so that their men could come aboard.

I was standing near the bows with Adam as the ship drew closer. "What kind of a vessel is this?" he wondered out loud. "She has too many guns for her length … and apart from the man at the helm there are just three on the deck. Where are the rest of the crew?"

As if to answer Adam's question, one of them forthwith drew a pistol he had hidden in his shirt and fired it into the air. At this signal, the ship's hatches flew

open and out rushed a
swarm of the fiercest men
I have ever seen. All of them
carried weapons – short
swords, pistols, knives, axes.
Each either screamed curses as he ran, or uttered a
piercing yell. Before leaping aboard our ship, the first of
them hurled what looked like a small, round, heavy jug
on to the deck. It smashed, and from it burst a puff of
grey, foul-smelling smoke. The cloud quickly hid the
deck from view, but aloft I could see that the PIRATES
(for so they proved to be) had hauled down their Dutch
flag, and hoisted a black flag with an hourglass and
crossed swords on it. Their topmen were also hard at
work, lashing together the yard-arms of the two ships,
which were touching.

"Damn your eyes, you treacherous rogues, STOP
THEM!" Our captain's voice cut through the smoke and
the pirates' yells. "Make sail! Make sail! Steer hard to port!"

As the smoke drifted away I could see that the crewmen close by seemed not to hear his words. To my puzzlement they merely stepped back as the pirates boarded.

The first to leap across was a tall, red-bearded man dressed in a fine frock-coat. He led a crowd of perhaps twenty pirates towards the quarterdeck. There had been some half-dozen people on it before the attack began. Now all were gone except our captain and second mate. The pair of them had drawn their swords and pistols. They slashed defiantly at the onrushing crowd, but the fight was too uneven by far. In moments they were surrounded, and their hands tied. But the men tying them up were not the pirates – they were OUR OWN CREW taking them captive!

Monday 22nd

The pirates have taken over our ship. They say it is in better repair than their own, and fast enough until they find a better prize. After the attack, half their number stayed aboard the *Greyhound* and sailed it to an anchorage, where we ride as I write this.

Most of my shipmates are delighted at the ship's capture. As one put it, "Now the flogging will stop." Indeed, this – and fear for their lives – explains why they did all but welcome the pirates aboard.

Not everyone is pleased, though. Bart, our boatswain, speaks bitterly of the pirates. Today, as he checked the sails, rigging and anchor (for these are a boatswain's tasks on the ship), he spoke thus to anyone who would listen: "They are just common thieves. Had we not joined them they would have murdered every one of us, yes, as easily as you or I would cut the head off a fish."

Noah argued with him: "That's all very well, Bart, but look at the way old Nick cast Will adrift. Was that not murder too? And is our captain less of a thief? He keeps back half our pay. If we jump ship we have not a penny. Yet if we stay aboard we are slaves."

Bart shook his head at this, but most murmured their agreement with Noah. For myself, I could not decide who was right or wrong. However, I fancy I will not need to choose, for the pirates outnumber us two to one, and they permit no opposition.

Tuesday 23rd

Today the pirates called all the *Greyhound*'s crew up on the deck and asked about the character and temper of the captain. Nobody spoke well of him and Thomas, the seaman who had been flogged, showed the weals on his back. Noah urged me forward to tell how my uncle was set adrift. I did not want to speak, for if I had not lost the bucket overboard Will might still be with us. But the pirate captain encouraged, "Come lad, don't be shy. Help us to decide what to do with the captain and second mate. Should we let them take charge again?" This so angered me that I shouted, "NO! Let them suffer the same punishment as my uncle did!"

Despite the discussions lasting most of the day, we are still none the wiser as to what will be done.

Wednesday 24th

We slaughtered and butchered Dan's goat today. It was a stinking nuisance when alive, but the goat's flesh made a fine stew – a welcome change from dried fish and meat. Our cook gave Abraham the skin, and I helped him tie it stretched out tight to dry. He aims to make jerkins for both of us from it.

The pirates have locked away all our weapons, and now sit idly on the deck smoking pipes, talking and drinking – which they do to great excess – from a barrel of rum which they took from our hold. In pirates' slang there are one hundred words for "drunk" and just one for "sober". Our own crew made willing drinking partners.

Bart alone sits apart and clucks his tongue (though even he sneaked a drink from the barrel).

Monday 29th

This day the pirates took from their leaky old tub such sails, ropes, cannon and equipment as they could easily remove. When all was stripped they fired the ship. The tar-soaked wood blazed down to the waterline. What was left sank with a roar and a hiss.

I can write no more, for we have been told to cut extra gunports in the side of the *Greyhound*, and as Adam's servant I help in this.

Tuesday 30th

Now that we have three times as many people on board, the ship is very crowded. It is worst at night, when the lower deck becomes loud with snores and the air grows thick and heavy. I awoke this morning with a taste in my mouth as if I had slept with a penny in it.

NOVEMBER
Sunday 4th

In the short battle to capture the *Greyhound*, a ball from the second mate's pistol found its mark and smashed the shin of Ahab, one of the pirates. Already the wound has maggots and unless his leg is cut off below the knee, he will surely die. All agreed that Adam would make the best surgeon, because he is handy with a saw. "Shall you help me, Jake?" he asked me. I agreed, but at once regretted it, for he went on to say, "Good, for after I have cut through a vein I shall need someone to press a red-hot poker against it. That will stop most of the blood and keep Ahab from bleeding to death. You can catch the rest of the blood in a bucket."

Though Ahab drank a pint of rum to dull the pain, he howled so loud when the sawing began that I swear the very fish on the sea bottom must have heard him. Adam was a good choice: he took the leg off in less than two minutes and dipped the stump in hot tar to stop the rest of the blood and help the leg heal. However, Adam now complains that his saw was made to cut wood, and that cutting bone has dulled its blade.

Tuesday 6th

Ahab died in the night. Bart sat with him to the end, dabbing his brow. He also read him comforting passages from the Bible, saying that "Even a pirate who is full of sin may be saved." Methinks that Ahab heard not a word of the Good Book, but his death certainly affected Bart. He now seems less opposed than he was to all of Ahab's shipmates.

Bart sewed up poor Ahab in sail-cloth with cannonballs at his head and feet. For the last stitch he passed the needle through the soft flesh between Ahab's nostrils. "That's to make sure he be really dead," he told me, "for the pain of the stitch would surely wake him if he were just asleeping."

Bart read a short prayer, and when all had said "Amen" they tipped poor Ahab into the ocean. The weights in his canvas coffin sank him quick.

Now we set sail again for Martinique, aiming to sell our cargo there as we had first planned.

Wednesday 7th

When I went below deck this forenoon to fill a bucket with water to wash the deck, I heard voices coming from the stern. The pirates were in the Great Cabin on the deck above. They were discussing what to do with our captain. By standing on a barrel directly below them I could hear every word. One said angrily, "Hang him from the topsail yard? Too kind! Let us slit open his belly."

This made me gasp, and one of them must have heard me, for he hissed, "Hush, someone listens…" All were silent for a moment, then to my relief they began again. A softer voice said, "Wicked he may be, and perhaps he deserves to be tortured and killed. But remember, one of us has to do the deed. Jim – you want to spill his guts on the deck. Will it be your knife that opens his belly?"

Again the cabin was quiet, so it was my guess Jim did not want this murderous job. "Well then, unless this man's ill-used crew will do the bloody business, I propose we maroon him."

This last bit I did not understand, but before I could learn more, a big wave tilted the ship and I fell from the barrel with a cry.

I knew from the thunder of feet above that I was

discovered. I dived behind some barrels and tried to curl myself out of sight. However, I was soon spotted. "There, over there! There is the scoundrel who dares spy on us!"

The pirates gathered around me in the gloom. Two had their pistols drawn and cocked. A huge and hairy hand lifted me from my hiding place and set me atop a barrel. Someone chuckled. "Why, 'tis the carpenter's lad!"

Stooping, the huge pirate captain brought his face so close to mine that his red whiskers tickled my chin. "So," he whispered, "you have heard what some of us would like to do to your captain?" I nodded. "Well, you wouldn't want to suffer the same fate, would you now?" Before I had time to open my mouth or shake my head, he bellowed, "Then BE OFF with you!" and knocked me from my perch. Thus I escaped, as scared as a rabbit in a snare, but otherwise not harmed.

Friday 16th

Two days ago our ship moored off the shore of a deserted island. The captain and second mate are still tied together in the hold.

We feasted on turtles today, for here they are plentiful. I ate more than was wise, and crept away to my hammock feeling quite ill.

Sunday 18th

We went ashore today to collect fresh water. However, there was a dispute over where we should draw it. Noah, our first mate, wished to look for a spring further inland. "The water of a spring," he told us, "is always pure. That of a stream is just as clear and tastes as sweet, but a dead animal in a pool upstream can make it unsafe to drink." Ben, the pirate captain, would have none of this, and at his command we fetched water from the first stream we found.

Tuesday 20th

We left the island today, but not before leaving behind the captain and second mate. This is the meaning of "marooning" that I heard the pirates speak of in their meeting.

As the pirates pushed them roughly from the boat into the surf, they handed the two men a musket, some lead balls and a horn of powder. I shrank back, fearing they would load the gun and shoot at us as we rowed from the beach. This made the men pulling on the oars laugh. "Why should they shoot at us?" they asked me. "They shall need every scrap of powder for shooting birds and wild goats to fill their bellies!"

When we returned to the ship we fired off a couple of cannon to celebrate being rid of Nick and Dan at last. One of our crewmen could play the fiddle and he struck up a merry tune while we danced a jig upon the deck.

My new goatskin jerkin makes me look smart enough – but now I smell like Dan's goat!

Thursday 22nd

Today we drew water from the barrel we had filled on the island, and those who drank from it soon became ill. The pirate crew called the illness "el vomito" as the Spanish do. Though we do not have a physician aboard there was no shortage of cures suggested. Abraham had this: "My grandmother always said moss scraped from the skull of a murderer was by far the best cure." Others proposed drinking pearls dissolved in wine or a poultice of pigeon dung. Fortunately we had none of these cures on the ship, and anyway, those who suffered recovered quickly after they had been sick.

Sunday 25th

The life of a pirate is not like that of a sailor on an ordinary ship. There, everyone must obey the captain without question. But this is not so among pirates. The whole company (which is what the pirates call those who sail together on their ship) chooses the captain and other officers. And though the captain commands the ship, the crew may replace him with another if enough disagree with his orders.

Those that fell ill were still aggrieved with Ben's decision on where to draw the water, so today we all picked a new captain. We chose between Noah, our first mate, and the pirate captain Ben. Even though the pirates outnumbered us, Noah was chosen, which pleased me greatly. Ben was a poor loser, and gave Noah an evil look. Though Noah will lead us, the pirates' boatswain Saul shall have this same office on the *Greyhound*, for our own boatswain Bart is still a most reluctant pirate.

Now we have a larger company and a new captain, the whole crew swore an oath of loyalty. As one of the few crew members who can write, it fell to me to draft the oath. I wrote it in the ship's log, and we all made our mark at the bottom of the page. There were ten "articles" (or rules) to which we swore.

1. EVERY MAN shall obey civil commands.

2. THE CAPTAIN shall have one full share and a half in all prizes; the carpenter and boatswain shall have one and a quarter. All others shall have one share.

3. A MAN that does not keep clean his weapons fit for an engagement, or otherwise neglects his business, shall be cut off from his share and suffer such other punishment as the company chooses.

4. IF A MAN shall lose a limb in time of an engagement he shall have 800 pieces of eight; if a lesser part, 400.

5. IF AT ANY TIME we should meet another pirate ship, any man that signs its articles without the consent of our company shall suffer such punishment as the captain and company think fitting.

6. IF ANY MAN shall attempt to run away, or keep any secret from the company, he shall be marooned with one bottle of water, one of powder, one small

arm and enough lead shot.

7. IF ANY MAN shall steal anything in the company worth more than a piece of eight, he shall be marooned or shot.

8. A MAN that strikes another shall receive Moses' law (39 lashes) on his bare back.

9. A MAN that discharges his pistol, or smokes tobacco in the hold, or carries a candle without the protection of a lantern, or otherwise risks fire on board, shall receive the same punishment.

10. IF AT ANY TIME a man meets with a prudent woman and offers to meddle with her without her consent, he shall suffer death.

The pirates take these rules most seriously, for they draw them up and agree to them amongst themselves. Many are deserters from the English, French and Dutch navies. On naval ships, petty rules govern even the smallest things and sailors are cruelly punished for breaking them.

On their own ship (leastways the one they have stolen) the pirates make their own laws, and they respect these above laws made by others.

DECEMBER
Monday 17th

Our ship has been sailing against the wind these past three weeks. To make a league's progress forward, we must sail many leagues to port, then go about (which means change direction) and sail the same distance to starboard! Zigzag sailing like this is called "tacking" or "wearing". This last word could not be truer; we are all utterly worn out from working the sails each time we turn.

Tuesday 25th, Christmas Day

I was looking forward to this festival, but I was surprised to find that not everyone on board celebrates this day. To the Dutchmen it was just another day (for *they* celebrate Christmas on January 5th). The English and French sailors made it an excuse for merrymaking and much drinking of rum. Seeing this, Bart said, "You will all burn in Hell's ovens!" He disapproves of such jollity, and marked the festival with several prayers.

JANUARY
Wednesday 9th

Last night we all slept not a wink, for we were tortured by a mournful song that seemed to come from the ocean's depths. The sailors on deck could hardly hear it, but the sound echoed plainly through the hull below.

Thursday 10th

During the afternoon the lookout pointed to the starboard side and shouted, "A monster! A great sea monster!" I rushed to look, and saw the tail of a giant fish thrash at the water, then disappear into the deep. Moments later the beast's gigantic body rose to the surface, and into the air blew a spout of water as tall as

two men. The fish was swimming quickly at our ship and I feared it would eat us in a single gulp. But when my shipmates saw my terror, it amused them greatly. One sailor called to me, "Fear not, lad, 'tis only a whale. I've hunted many of these beasts in the icy waters up north." However, at that moment a huge fin appeared from the waves, fully twenty feet in length. It crashed into the ship's side, shaking every timber, and took away a section of deck rail before the beast dived from sight.

Saturday 12th

Today we arrived at a small island to careen the ship – that is scraping from her bottom the barnacles and weed that slow our progress through the water. While we are here we shall also repair the damage done by the whale.

First we unloaded the cargo (apart from the disgusting salt fish which remains for the cook to use). From the timber we were carrying we built a stockade. Then we loaded the barrels within it and covered it with old sails taken from the pirate ship. This will serve as our warehouse while we look for a richer prize. To hide it from prying eyes we covered the whole with sand from the dunes.

Next, the *Greyhound* was anchored in shallow water at high tide, and we secured everything on board. When the tide went out the *Greyhound* was left high and dry on the shore and we propped her up with timbers for the work.

Saturday 26th

Careening and repairing the ship has taken these last two weeks. There was much to do so everyone lent a hand, but still it was a tiresome task. I would never have guessed that so much of the hull lay below the water. After the hull was scraped clean, we coated the ship in a foul-smelling mixture of grease and brimstone, to protect against the plants and tiny sea beasties returning. Adam and I also replaced any broken or rotted planks.

Places to careen a ship are few, for there must be a

beach both sandy and steep. So it was no surprise when another pirate ship, the *Ranger*, arrived with the same purpose in mind. This led to some merry carousing, and the story of the sea monster greatly improved in the retelling.

Sunday 27th

We learned from the *Ranger* that a fleet of treasure ships bound for Spain sank off the Florida shore last summer. The Spaniards are using divers to raise from the wrecks gold and other treasure! Everything they find, they carry ashore each night for safe-keeping. Pirate leader Henry Jennings is planning an attack on the Spanish camp. The *Ranger* is to join him, and we have agreed to follow!

Monday 28th

We challenged the *Ranger* to a cannon contest today. There was a serious intent behind this sport. Noah wanted to be sure that we could fight as well as we could sail.

Each man has but one job when firing a gun. I am a powder monkey. I run to the lower deck to fetch gunpowder. It is stored there in a "magazine", a cabin protected by curtains of wet canvas against sparks that fly in a battle. Inside, the gunner packs enough powder for each shot into a paper parcel. This we call a "charge".

I take the charge and carry it in a leather box to the cannon. Abraham, who has the same job, warned me, "Be careful! If a spark lights it, the powder will surely blow us both to atoms."

The rest of the gun-crew works thus. The loader puts the charge into the barrel of the cannon, then some cloth to keep the charge in place, and finally the ball.

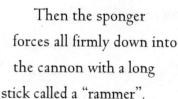

Then the sponger forces all firmly down into the cannon with a long stick called a "rammer".

The gun captain then cuts the charge by pushing a small spike into the touch hole at the closed end of the gun. He then calls "Run out!" and all eight of the gun-crew haul on the ropes to pull the gun to the gunport.

The gun captain holds a glowing taper to the touch hole and the ball is fired with a deafening crash.

The *Ranger* was the first to hit the target and won the contest. However, our gun-crew is the fastest on the *Greyhound*. We can load and fire our piece in less than a minute.

Tuesday 29th

At last we set sail, bound for the coast of Florida, where we shall meet Henry Jennings – and the Spanish treasure!

FEBRUARY
Monday 4th

We have reached Florida, and have been joined by three ships. Henry Jennings, who now leads our small army of 300 pirates, calls us "The Flying Gang". A boat rowed him over, and I learned from one of his oarsmen that the three ships come from a place called New Providence, an island only a couple of days' sailing from here. One of our crew who has been there tells me, "It is a paradise, where pirates do as they please without fear of the law."

Wednesday 6th

It was not difficult to find the Spanish as their ships are anchored above the wrecks. The crews sleep ashore, which is scarce two hundred yards distant, leaving a couple of sailors on watch on the ships.

The moon had not yet risen, and we doused all lights except those that shone to seaward. Thus hidden by the night we could sail close in to the shore; so close, in fact, that we could see the fires of the Spaniards' camp and hear the music they were playing. The sailors left on watch must have been drinking too, as they did not espy our approach.

At first, the crew favoured leaving me on board the ship during the raid. They thought I was still too much of a landsman to risk on such a venture, but I pleaded with them to take me. Eventually my begging had some effect, for Noah told me he had found me a task. "Very well, Jake. You shall guard the boats on the shore until we return." I guessed that this safe work was chosen because of my age. I did not protest but instead I secretly resolved to follow them to the camp.

With this in mind, I took two pistols which one of the pirates had left behind on his hammock-roll. The pistols were too small for the owner's purpose but suited me well, so I hid them in my belt. I was able to load them easily (I watched how others did it) and powder and ball were free for all before we set off.

Leaving our ships riding at anchor, we quietly rowed ashore. A whistle-blast was the signal for our attack. When it came, we sprang upon the Spanish from the shadows. Most fled like frightened rabbits, but not their capitano. He fought so boldly that no one could get near him.

Our boatswain Saul knelt down and aimed his musket at the tall figure now alone in the centre of the camp. He pulled the trigger; the flint snapped, the powder flashed, but alas, the gun did not fire. The flash, though, attracted the attention of the capitano. Saul rose and drew his sword, but lost his footing on the soft sand and tumbled awkwardly to the ground.

In a moment the capitano was on top of him, and stood in his heavy sea boots on the sleeves of Saul's coat, pinning him to the ground. He laughed in triumph as he cocked his two pistols and pointed both at Saul's head.

A blinding flash of light and a deafening blast engulfed me. I had never fired a pistol before, let alone two at once. I was so dazed that I was hardly aware of what happened next. Saul told me that one of my pistol balls flew wide of the mark, but the other hit the capitano's shoulder; thus was Saul's life spared and the capitano quickly captured. His wound was slight, and before we returned to our ships we left him tied to a tree.

Friday 8th

Our attack worked better than any of us dreamed it could. I was a hero (for a day, at least) and was forgiven for "forgetting" Noah's orders to guard the boats and my "borrowing" of the pistols. Without loss of any of our

number we captured 350,000 pieces of eight. Henry Jennings counted the coins out into piles on a table in his Great Cabin. He distributed to each his share, but only after taking dice from us, so that we would not gamble it away. For my part I was given 564 of the coins – a small fortune, and more than my father ever had in his life.

MARCH
Tuesday 12th

Last night I felt more afeared than I ever have since the pirates attacked our ship. Every crew member takes turns on deck watching for danger. I was on middle watch, and thus took my turn in the dead of night. It was cloudy and the sky was black as treacle. As I listened to the creaking timbers, it seemed to me that our ship was alive, breathing and sighing as she pitched in the ocean swell. Worse still, a storm gathered and the upper rigging began to glow with an unearthly light.

I dreaded that the ship was doomed and would be consumed by fire from the sky. I cried out loud, and my alarm brought the gunner (who was also on watch) to my side. He quickly calmed me saying, "Hush Jake, we're all safe. The flames in the rigging are a kind of lightning. There's even a name for them: Saint Elmo's fire." Then he told me that this saint is the guardian of sailors and that I should call on him when I feared harm.

After our successful raid we fled quickly, but now, safe from fear of capture by Spanish warships, most of the crew seem content to do nothing. Adam, however, cannot bear to be idle, so today we went in search of leaks to plug. He called over, "Pass me the Dutch saw, lad; the small 'un." I looked, but could find it nowhere in his bag. We searched the hold and tool store, but the saw had vanished. Adam said, "A wave must have taken it while my back was turned." I worry he does not believe this and suspects that I have lost it – which I have not!

Friday 15th

Today I learned about another of the sea's mysteries. Through the mist we heard a strange chirping song. Then I heard the helmsman gasp, "Look! A mermaid!" Sure enough, there she sat on a sandbank. I had heard of these creatures, half fish, half woman, but I doubted they existed. Now I have seen one, I am still not certain who – or what – they are.

As we all looked, a debate started up. "'Tis a mermaid, no doubt about it," said one. "Nay, man!" said another. "Mermaids are young and beautiful and sit combing their long, blonde hair. This lass is bald, ugly and old. Why, she even has long whiskers, and is as big as a carthorse."

I could not decide who was right. I glimpsed her for just a moment, and then the mist hid the sandbank from view.

Tuesday 19th

The other pirate ships having gone on their way, we set sail today for the pirate island in the Bahamas. A misadventure delayed us. Noah is in the habit of leaning against the deck rail and smoking a pipe of tobacco. He always chooses the same spot for this relaxation.

Today, as he rested there, the rail gave way and he plunged overboard. The *Greyhound* was in a flat calm, so we were able to lower a boat and recover him from the water. He was shaken, and the fall had hurt his arm, but he came to no real harm.

Things would have been different indeed had we been under way in a stiff breeze. Then he would have been two leagues astern by the time we had brought the *Greyhound* to a halt.

When we studied the rail we saw it had been cut three-fourths through, and pitch smeared over it to hide the cut. 'Twas clear that it was someone's evil intent the rail break, and not an accident. Noah might have suspected Adam if he did not know that the Dutch saw had disappeared a week past. Since none but the thief knew who had taken the saw, each eyed his companions with suspicion. This is a bad thing on a ship, for the sea is a dangerous place. A hundred times a day you must trust your life on knots your shipmates have tied.

Friday 22nd

The journey to New Providence is just 200 miles and – aside from Noah's mishap – has so far passed without incident. For the first time since I put to sea I found myself bored.

Some of my companions pass the time by carving sea monsters' teeth into fantastic shapes, or by engraving pictures on them. Adam showed me two coconuts that he had carved and polished to make a drinking cup and a container for tobacco.

Gabriel and Pierre struck up a merry tune on the whistle and fiddle and many of the company danced a jig or two around the deck.

One of the seamen, who has hunted whales in the north, passes the time by decorating the skin of his messmates in a manner he learned from the Eskimo people. He pierces their skin with a needle, and pulls a thread rolled in soot through the bloody hole. This looks very painful and I quickly turned down the offer to have myself decorated likewise!

Bart scoffs at all this recreation, calling it "a waste of time". He spends his idle hours sewing clothes for himself and for others who are not as skilled with a needle as he. When he is finished with this industry he carves tools for splicing and covering ropes – that is joining and wrapping them in canvas to protect them. He showed me two: a fid and a serving mallet.

Sunday 24th

We reached New Providence this morning. Within its large harbour are upwards of four score ships. We took great care sailing into the harbour, to avoid colliding with the pirates, slavers and contrabandists moored everywhere. We handed all the sails, put out the large oars (called sweeps), and carefully rowed the *Greyhound* until we found space to anchor.

It is exactly as I had been told it would be. There are just a few shacks, but the sand dunes have become a town of tents. Their ragged owners sell or rent everything imaginable, from ships' provisions and hardware to wine and rum.

Monday 25th

To go ashore, we had to leap from the rowing boat and wade a little way through the surf. I waited my turn behind Ben (who was the pirate captain until we chose Noah). He jumped into the water, then turned back to get his bag. As he lifted it, something shiny clattered into the boat. I called out, "Wait, Ben! You've dropped something!" We all stared into the bottom of the boat –

and there lay the Dutch saw Adam had lost! When I turned to look back at Ben, he had made a run for it. We started after him, but Noah shook his head. "Let him go. We are better off without the rat. I suspected it was he who cut the rail, but as I could prove nothing, I judged it better to say nothing."

APRIL
Wednesday 3rd

Today some unexpected news caused great excitement on the island! From a ship out of Bermuda we learn that September last, England's King George declared an Act of Grace, aiming to bring an end to piracy. Those pirates who swear to give up their trade shall receive a royal pardon, and will not be punished. This is good news, since (as is well known) the punishment for piracy is usually execution by the hangman's noose.

The governor of Bermuda had sent his man here to read the Act, and a huge crowd gathered. I could scarcely hear as the wind carried away the man's words. Nevertheless, it was easy to learn what he said, for since then the talk has been of nothing else.

Friday 5th

The pardon has split our company. The navy deserters in our crew oppose it for they say that "Pardon or no pardon, we will be forced once more on to battleships." There are also among us those who hate England's king and despise all his laws and pardons. Some of the company have known no other life but piracy, and others have taken a liking to their new occupation. As one of them told me, "The life of an ordinary sailor, fisherman or farmer seems a dull one now."

Many of us, though, welcome the king's forgiveness. We all have Spanish silver in our pockets (leastways, those of us who had not lost it at cards among the dunes of New Providence), and a pardon would free us from the fear of capture by the king's men.

However, there is a problem. We need to go to a colonial port to be pardoned. If those who favour a pardon sail away in the *Greyhound*, how shall the remainder go a-pirating? And if the pirates take the ship, how shall the others return?

Wednesday 10th

Our company has reached an agreement. Altogether, those who wish to continue with the piratical life number just ten. The remainder, who want the king's pardon, shall take the ship. In payment for the *Greyhound* each forfeits one-fourth of their share of the silver.

I have decided to take the pardon. I fear that if I were to stay a pirate I might never see my father again. And if I were caught and hanged, it would bring great shame on my family.

Parting with a quarter of my share of the Spanish silver seems a high price to pay. However, when we reach our destination we aim to sell the ship, and thus recover our losses.

Friday 26th

Greyhound set sail for Bath town on the Pamlico river. We dare not return to Charleston. Old Nick owed every merchant there money, and we fear they would take the ship in settlement of the debts. Abraham, Adam, Bart and Noah sail with us, as do thirty others.

I cannot say I am sorry to leave New Providence

behind. Some cherish the island as a pirates' paradise, but I shall best remember the stench of the place and the rats (which surely outnumbered the people).

MAY
Saturday 11th

Yesterday, after sighting land, we ran into a storm. Noah had been studying the sky since dawn yesterday, and he had looked uneasy all morning. Just before noon he commanded abruptly, "Shorten sail!" This surprised us, for the weather seemed fair, with a good following wind. Every one of us was keen to return to shore with all possible haste; but by rolling up the canvas we would sail more slowly. An argument broke out, and Noah was called "a futtock-kneed old fool", but our captain would not be moved.

We went aloft and shortened sail until there were just three sails spread before the wind. However, there was much grumbling on the yard-arm, where Noah could not hear. No sooner had we returned to the deck when the wind veered rapidly round. Half-an-hour later, we spied black clouds moving in from the east.

"Get the anchor ready! Cook, douse the fire!" cried out Noah. Hearing this, we feared the worst, for clearly he was expecting a sea strong enough to throw the embers from the hearth. "Topmen, shorten sail!" The topmen hurried aloft while on the deck the rest of us hauled the thick anchor cable from its locker. Soon we had only two small staysails set, yet still the wind drove us on through the rising waves faster than a galloping horse.

Noah beckoned to a topman standing nearby, and pointed at the sails. "Take some men aloft and hand those last two." Then to Saul our boatswain: "Stand clear of the cable and let go anchor."

Though he was
just a few paces
away, Noah had
to yell the
words to be
heard above the

storm. The anchor dropped into the ocean, and the thick
cable snaked from its coils on the deck. It scarcely
seemed to halt our progress.

I looked with alarm at the shore, for we were now
close enough to see the waves breaking on the treacherous sandbars, and the wind was forcing us closer each
minute.

Our brave topmen were handing the last sail when
the storm struck. The wind plucked the sail from their
hands and hurled it into the foaming ocean. Two of the
topmen had lashed themselves on to the yard-arm, but
the third had not, and he followed the sail into the sea.
We could do nothing to save him. By now, each of us

had only one thought: to save himself.

Gigantic waves crashed over the deck, shaking the ship as if each one was a great hammer. I heard Saul shout to Noah, "The anchor's dragging! I'll let go the sheet anchor." This is a reserve anchor, used only in the direst emergencies. But even with two anchors out we were still driving towards the shore.

The ship let out a terrible groan, as if in pain, and there was a mighty crash from above. Looking up, I saw that the storm had snapped the main topmast in two as easily as snapping twigs for kindling, though it is as thick as my waist.

When I saw this I was sure we would all perish, but soon after this catastrophe the storm quieted a little, and then, an hour or so later, it suddenly passed on, leaving the *Greyhound* riding at anchor just a mile from the Carolina shore.

We worked the pumps to drain some of the water that the storm had dashed into the *Greyhound*; Saul also checked and secured what was left of the rigging. Thus satisfied that the ship was safe, we all dragged ourselves to our hammocks, exhausted by the storm. I write these words soon after sun-up, while others are yet asleeping around me. As soon they awake, we shall all have much to do if we are to get under way before nightfall.

Sunday 12th

We have still not finished repairing the damage done by Tuesday's storm, but we cannot safely continue until the work is done. The falling topmast brought down with it the upper topsail yards. As it tumbled, this stout timber smashed one of the boats stored on the deck and broke several of the rope stays which hold the masts upright. The boat is beyond repair, but we replaced most of the damaged stays with the spare cordage from the hold. The topmen have spliced together the remainder. Adam and I were kept busy about the deck, making good the smashed rails and other timbers.

The rest of the crew took turns at the pumps. The falling topmast smashed one of the hatches, and thus the sea entered the hold in great amounts. Worse though, the storm so twisted and turned the ship that many seams opened. Without constant pumping the *Greyhound* will founder and sink before the day is out.

Monday 13th

Our repairs are completed today, and we set sail once more. We cannot replace the topmast at sea, but we can spread enough canvas on the yards that remain to make good progress. Noah has decided it is not safe to sail for Bath town port, for it is yet sixty leagues away. Instead, we must return to Charleston, which we shall reach tomorrow, God willing.

Tuesday 14th

By noon today we had sailed up the Ashley river and reached Charleston harbour. As we sailed closer, we saw a grim scene. At the end of the quay, just by the harbour light, stood a crude wooden frame, its timbers bleached white by the sun and sea. Hanging from the frame was an iron cage, shaped like a man. And inside the cage was a man – at least, what was left of a man, though 'twas hardly more than greasy bones wrapped in rags. As I watched, a seagull landed on the cage and pecked at the skull. "It's Jack Rattenbury," said a voice behind me. "He was hanged for piracy two months back. That's a friendly

87

Englishman's way of making an example of those who break their king's laws." After this, we were all silent until the *Greyhound* tied up at the quayside.

The customs searchers were waiting for us. They descended into the ship and had just begun to search the crew's possessions when Noah dropped a purse full of pieces of eight – some ten for each searcher. As none of us stirred to pick up the coins, the searchers guessed that Noah's clumsiness was no accident. Gathering the silver, they cut short their visit. Before stepping ashore, though, they warned us that we should present ourselves at the customs house on Friday to swear an oath of loyalty to the king of England, as the Act of Grace requires us.

Friday 17th

Today our company went to the customs house on the quayside. There, each of us stepped up, one by one, before Governor Johnson. A member of his council read the oath from a piece of paper and we repeated the words after he said them. When my turn came, the governor bent down and stared me in the eye. "What's your name, lad?" he asked me. When I told him, he said, "I am most relieved that you have forsworn piracy. You will no longer be a threat to South Carolina or a danger to the good people of Charleston." This remark caused much mirth and laughter.

Every one of us got a letter to prove that we had promised to be pirates no longer, and we returned to the ship. Tomorrow, though, I must seek lodgings. Charleston merchants have got wind of our return and, as we guessed, they have taken the *Greyhound* and will auction her off to get what they are owed.

Monday 20th

I feel quite alone now, for this morning I bade farewell to Abraham and the others. They have all signed up with another merchant ship and left port today. I was tempted to go with them, until I heard that their cargo is salt fish!

I shall miss Abraham especially, for he has been a good friend these last few months.

I shall set off home tomorrow to Holyoak to see my father. He will be most surprised to see me – and my treasure!

Tuesday 21st

This day I had such a wondrous surprise that I cannot believe my good fortune! I had gone for one last look at the *Greyhound*, when I heard someone call out my name. To my astonishment it was my Uncle Will! I had thought him certainly dead, but there he was, as alive as I am.

"I drifted for three days in that little boat, Jake," he told me later, "until fishermen rescued me. The flogging had left my back like a piece of raw meat, but in time it healed." When he was well he had journeyed to

Charleston hoping to find work. "I heard that the *Greyhound* was in the port, and came to see if you were still among the crew."

We had much to talk about, and I swear Will did not believe my stories until I showed him this journal and my purse. When we had finished our yarns, we considered whether to buy a farm with my Spanish silver. This we discounted, for we agreed we would miss the sea. I told him of the creek where we had careened the ship, and we pondered whether to sail there and salvage the buried cargo. We rejected this plan too, for the rice was not really ours to claim, and I have left piracy behind me now. Tiredness ended our debate without a decision.

Wednesday 22nd

Will and I have chosen to return home, but then
to travel north to join the crew of a fishing ship in
Newfoundland. They say you can dip your hat overboard
there, and haul it out filled with fish. My bag is packed
and we leave forthwith; Will is shouting for me. Who
knows when I will next have time to continue my journal?

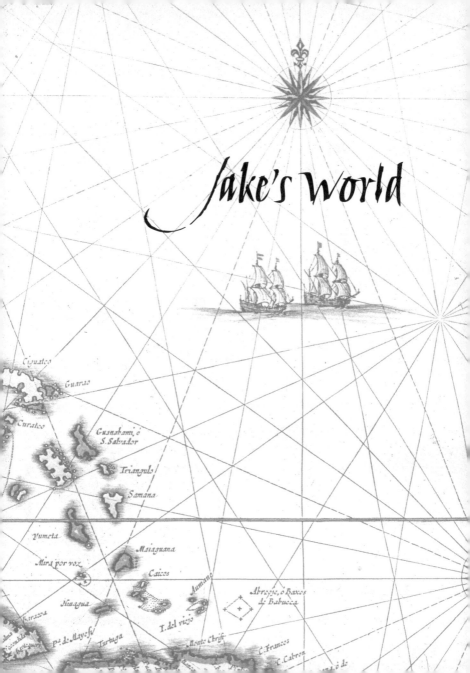

Jake's World

MAP OF JAKE'S JOURNEY

NORTH AMERICA

Charleston

ATLANTIC OCEAN

FLORIDA

WEST INDIES

CUBA

MARTINIQUE

CARIBBEAN SEA

N

KEY TO THE MAP

1 CHARLESTON: Jake sets sail on board the *Greyhound*.

2 ATTACK: The *Greyhound* is attacked by pirates.

3 MAROONING: Captain Nick and Daniel left here.

4 CAREENING: The ship is repaired and meets the *Ranger*.

5 TREASURE: Henry Jennings's raid on the Spanish camp.

6 NEW PROVIDENCE: Jake hears of the Act of Grace.

7 STORM: The *Greyhound* is thrown off course and damaged.

8 HOME: Back in Charleston and reunited with Will.

JAKE'S DIARY is a story, but the things he describes are true to life. Seamen really did become pirates to escape from the brutal treatment on merchant ships. But life was tough for landsmen too, and these hardships would bring about some dramatic changes.

The Colonies

Until he went to sea, Jake lived in a tiny village in North Carolina. It was not far from the south-east coast of what we would now call the United States. In 1716, though, North Carolina was a colony: a region of North America where European people had settled, starting about a century earlier.

North and South Carolina were British colonies. There were eleven others. Each was supposed to be an overseas part of Britain, but the settlers' loyalty to the country they

THE AMERICAN COLONIES

North Carolina

South Carolina

ATLANTIC OCEAN

had come from was often weak. Many had fled to America because in England they could not worship as they chose. Others came because the farmland was free or cheap. All, though, were independently minded people with strong ideas.

Life for the colonists was often harsh; cold, hunger and disease were constant threats. Some were killed by America's native people (on whose lands they built their farms). The British also had to fight off rival Spanish colonists. The Spanish wanted the land the British had settled, but the attacks were part of a wider battle. Since the beginning of the 18th century Britain had been at war with Spain and its ally, France.

Despite these problems, the thirteen colonies prospered. To make sure that Britain shared in their growing success, the government in London taxed and controlled the settlers' trade. A series of laws, called the Navigation Acts, forced them to trade only with England, using English ships with English crews.

Colonial people did not like the Navigation Acts, because the rules forced them to accept low prices for the goods they produced. Many colonists just ignored these unpopular laws. They sold their produce wherever they could get the best deal – even if this meant sailing to Caribbean ports occupied by the French, Britain's wartime foe. The colonists called it good business. The British government called it smuggling.

The people of South Carolina faced special difficulties. They suffered more than most from Spanish attacks, because they were closest to Spanish settlements in what is now the neighbouring state of Georgia. So they were enthusiastic supporters of the privateers – merchant seamen given permission by the king to attack Spanish shipping and settlements while the countries were at war.

Peace and Pirates

When Britain and Spain made peace in 1714, the raiders continued harassing the Spanish, but now illegally, as pirates. Many of the settlers were reluctant to turn their backs on those who had once protected them. They aided the pirates by supplying and repairing their ships. In return the pirates sold them their booty at knock-down prices.

This cosy arrangement worked well – until the pirates' customers tired of their wild manners and sickening violence, and no longer welcomed them in colonial ports and harbours. However, as piracy dwindled, anger about trade restrictions grew stronger. It flared into open rebellion some sixty years after Jake's voyage. In the War of Independence that followed, the thirteen colonies broke from Britain … and the United States of America was born.

A History of Piracy & the Lives of the Most Famous Rogues

The First Pirates

When the world's first sailors set off across the Mediterranean some 4,600 years ago, pirates were close behind.

They didn't have to look far. Cautious sailors kept their trading ships in sight of land. This made life simple for pirates, who just anchored close to the shore and waited for a ship to sail into sight.

Viking Raiders

The Mediterranean wasn't the only area threatened by pirates; they also attacked European coasts much farther north. Between the 9th and 11th centuries Viking sailors cruised the North Sea, the Atlantic and the Baltic from their Scandinavian homeland.

Travelling in light, fast ships they raided coastal towns and villages as far west as Ireland, and in the east, deep into Russia. Later, Vikings became settlers, founding peaceful colonies in lands they had once plundered.

Privateers

All these pirates, though, looked like amateurs compared to the rival nations of Europe and their fight for control of the seas. Their kings and queens could not afford to build navies; instead they used merchant ships as "men-of-war" – battleships. These vessels were called privateers, which was short for "private men-of-war". England's King Henry III was the first to use them, against the French, in the mid-13th century. He issued each privateer with a "letter of marque": a piracy permit. This authorized the captain of a merchant ship to attack the enemy on the king's behalf. King and captain each took half the spoils. In practice, many privateers went further. They didn't look too closely to see which country's flag flew from their victims' masts.

When war ended, privateers were supposed to return to their peacetime trade. However, raid and plunder were more profitable so many privateers carried on in peacetime just as they had in wartime – and became pirates.

Corsairs

Sixteenth-century Mediterranean pirates had a unique excuse for plunder: religion. Three centuries earlier Christians and Muslims had fought over the Holy Lands – the countries we now call Israel and Syria. Hatred still lingered, and from opposite shores of the Mediterranean supporters of each religion launched sleek, oared fighting ships called galleys to attack the other's shipping.

From the Muslim cities of Tunis, Algiers and Tripoli, galleys went to sea with Christian slaves chained to the oars. The pirates were called "corsairs" after the Latin word *cursus*, meaning plunder. When the corsairs captured Christian ships, they enslaved the crew and passengers. Those too weak to row were taken to work in slave prisons.

Christians launched counter-attacks from the island of Malta. Though their religion was different to that of the corsairs, their methods were the same: they used similar galleys, but with Muslim slaves at the oars.

BARBAROSSA BROTHERS
(c. 1474–1546)

Of all the Barbary corsairs, none were more famous than the Barbarossa brothers, Aruj (died 1518) and Khayr ad-Din (died 1546). These Greek Muslim pirates made Algiers a powerful corsair base in the early 16th century. Khayr ad-Din's exploits earned him promotion from corsair chief to commander of the Turkish navy, and he led raids on many ports in Spain, France and Italy. The name Barbarossa comes from the Latin words for red (*rossa*) and beard (*barba*).

New World Pirates

As the 16th century began, the world grew suddenly bigger. At least, it seemed so for Europeans, whose adventurers discovered a "New World" on the far side of the Atlantic. Spanish navigators led the exploration of the Caribbean. Moving on to the "Spanish Main" – mainland America – they plundered the wealth of two great native American peoples: the Incas of Peru, and the Aztecs of Mexico. As Spanish treasure ships transported their gold and silver back to Spain by the tonne, England's queen sent her privateers to capture them.

FRANCIS DRAKE
(c. 1540–1596)

One of England's best-known Elizabethan sailors, Francis Drake, turned pirate after the Spanish raided his merchant ship in the Caribbean.

Determined to teach them a lesson, he became a privateer. A 1572 attack on the Spanish town of Nombre de Dios in Panama made his reputation and a three-year raiding voyage around the world, ending in 1580, won him fame, wealth and a knighthood from England's queen, Elizabeth I. Sir Francis Drake died of a tropical disease off Panama during his last expedition in 1596.

Buccaneers

When Spain and England made peace in 1604, privateers could no longer legally raid Spanish ships. But before long a new, more brutal breed of pirate appeared: the buccaneers. Originally wild hunters from Hispaniola (now Haiti and the Dominican Republic), they were named after the "boucan" barbecues on which they smoked their meat. Passing sailors who bought the supplies called the hunters "boucaniers" and later buccaneers.

Hispaniola's Spanish rulers became alarmed by the lawless buccaneers, and sent an expedition to shoot all the animals they hunted. The buccaneers got their own back by raiding Spanish ships from their island base of Tortuga. Buccaneer quickly became another word for pirate.

Britain again went to war with Spain at the beginning of the 18th century, and privateers joined the buccaneers in raiding Spanish ships. When peace returned in 1714 they stayed on, and piracy exploded.

FRANÇOIS L'OLLONAIS
(1630–1668)

French pirate François L'Ollonais was a hunter on Hispaniola when Spaniards attacked his camp, killing his friends. By avenging their deaths he became the most savage of all the Caribbean buccaneers. In one particularly cruel incident he cut out the heart of one Spanish prisoner and fed it to another. L'Ollonais died as he had lived: captured by cannibals in Panama, he was cut to pieces, roasted and eaten.

HENRY MORGAN
(1635–1688)

Henry Morgan became a hero when he led small armies of buccaneers in daring raids on the Central American Spanish cities of Portobello in 1668

and Panama three years later. Morgan's drunken followers tortured and murdered during the attacks. Nevertheless, the English king, Charles II, later knighted the Welsh pirate for fighting England's enemy, and made him deputy governor of Jamaica!

Jake's Adventure

The pirate menace was so great in the 18th century that this period is sometimes called the golden age of piracy. This was the world that Jake strayed into when he signed on with the *Greyhound*.

Though Jake never really lived, some of the people he met did. Henry Jennings was a real pirate captain, and his raid on the Spanish salvage crew's camp actually took place. There was even a lawless pirate colony on New Providence – until it was broken up in 1718 by English former privateer Woodes Rogers. By using the English king's pardon for those who agreed to "retire", Woodes Rogers began a campaign that eventually ended piracy's golden age. In eight years pirate attacks fell from fifty to just six.

WILLIAM KIDD (c. 1645–1701)

When William Kidd sailed from England for the Indian Ocean in 1696, his aim was to capture pirates. His mission was a failure and, perhaps to satisfy his restless crew, he turned to piracy himself, seizing the Indian ship *Quedagh Merchant*. Kidd was hunted down, tried and hanged for piracy. His treasure, though, was never found, and according to legend it still lies buried on a Caribbean island.

HENRY AVERY (?–?)

British pirate Henry Avery is famous for a single spectacular – and brutal – raid. Cruising as admiral of a small pirate fleet in the Red Sea in 1695, he sighted the Indian treasure ship *Gang-I-Sawai*. After a fierce battle to capture the ship, Avery and his crew killed and mistreated many of the passengers. The pirates escaped with at least £325,000 worth of gold coins, jewels and trinkets such as a diamond-encrusted saddle – more than a lifetime's wages for each pirate. Despite a large reward, Avery was never caught.

BLACKBEARD *(?–1718)*

To terrify the crews of ships he attacked, English pirate

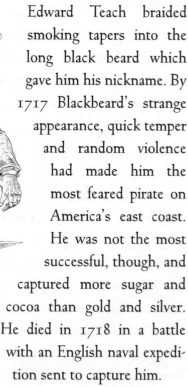

Edward Teach braided smoking tapers into the long black beard which gave him his nickname. By 1717 Blackbeard's strange appearance, quick temper and random violence had made him the most feared pirate on America's east coast. He was not the most successful, though, and captured more sugar and cocoa than gold and silver. He died in 1718 in a battle with an English naval expedition sent to capture him.

MARY READ (1690–1720) AND ANNE BONNY (?–?)

Mary Read and Anne Bonny wore men's clothes when they fought alongside the other pirates on "Calico" Jack Rackham's ship. However, whether or not their shipmates knew their true identity is still a mystery. Captured with the rest of the crew, Read and Bonny escaped execution by claiming to be pregnant.

JEAN LAFITTE (c.1780–c.1821)

Around 1810, glamorous American pirate Jean Lafitte built up a fleet of ten ships off the American coast near New Orleans. Lafitte's gang plundered British, Spanish and American ships while the United States government was distracted by the war of 1812. Later in the war Lafitte's pirates helped US forces defend New Orleans against the British foe. To thank him, the president offered to forgive his crimes, but Lafitte rejected the pardon and continued as a small-time pirate until his death.

Piracy Today

Piracy continues today, and those who live by it are as brutal as 17th-century buccaneers. Pirates operate in all the world's oceans, but the seas of East Asia are by far the most dangerous – two-thirds of all pirate attacks take place there.

Today's pirates either swoop quickly in fast boats, rob the crew of cash and small valuable items, and then flee, or occasionally they hijack ships to sell not only the cargo but the ship too. And they don't let sympathy for the crew stand in their way: when pirates hijacked the *Global Mars* in the Malacca Straits in February 2000, they forced the crew to flee in an open boat – just as Captain Nick set Will adrift in Jake's story.

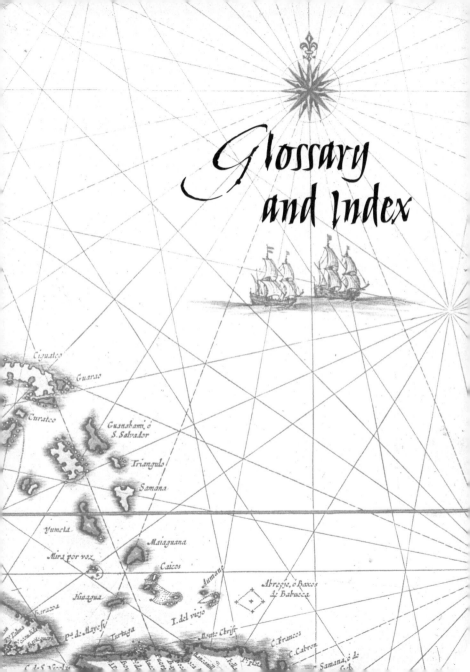

Glossary
and Index

Glossary and Index

Page numbers that are <u>underlined</u> show where unusual words which pirates would have used have already been explained – other unusual words are explained here. Words shown in *italics* have their own entries, with more information or pages to look up.

A

B

D

DECKS 12, 44 See also *lower deck*, *quarterdeck* and *upper deck*.

DESERTER 52, 76 A sailor or soldier that has run away from the navy or army. Captured deserters were punished very severely.

DOCK 17 A place by the side of a river or coast where ships could unload their *cargo*.

DRAKE, FRANCIS 105–106

E, F

EXECUTION 75, 78, 87, 109, 111

FID 73

FIRST MATE 23, 24

FLOGGING 26, 29, 38, 39, 90

FOOD 14, 20, 31, 40 See also *ship's biscuits*.

FORE 15

FOREMAST 5, 13, 31

FORENOON 44

FORESAIL 17 See also *sails*.

G

GALLEY 5, 20

GOAT 24, 40

GOLDEN AGE OF PIRACY 108

GOVERNOR 75, 88, 108 The ruler of a colony or state.

GREAT CABIN 5, 14, 23, 44, 68

GUN CAPTAIN 61 The leader of the *gun-crew*.

GUN-CREW 60–61

GUNNER 60

GUNPORT 41, 61 A hole cut into the sides of a ship for a *cannon* to fire through.

H

HAMMOCK 12, 14, 47

HANDING SAILS 21, 74

HARBOUR MASTER 10 An official in charge of a harbour.

HELM 33 The *tiller* or wheel used to steer the ship. See also *tiller*.

N

NAVIGATION
24, 27–29
NAVIGATION ACTS 99
NAVIGATOR 24
NEW PROVIDENCE 62, 71,
72–78, 96, 108

O

OARSMAN 62 A sailor who
rows one of the ship's boats.
OATH OF LOYALTY 51

P

PIECES OF EIGHT 52, 68, 88
The pirates' name for old
Spanish coins called pesos. Each
peso was worth eight reals
(another type of Spanish coin).
Pieces of eight were made of
silver and therefore very valuable.

PIRATE FLAG 36 Each pirate
captain had his own flag.
Common flag symbols included
skulls, swords and an hourglass
(to show victims their time was
running out).
PISS-DALE 25
PORT 15
POWDER MONKEY 60
PRIVATEER 100, 102–103, 105
PRIZE 38 A captured ship.
PUMPS 5, 26, 84, 86

Q

QUARTERDECK 5, 26, 37
The highest deck at the rear of a
ship. The ship's officers would
stand here.

R

RATS 32, 79
READ, MARY 111
REEFING SAIL 31
RIGGING 13, 38, 68, 85
ROGERS, WOODES 108

S

SAILS 13, 21, 38, 58, 81 See also *foresail* and *upper topsails*.

SAINT ELMO'S FIRE 69

SANDBAR 81 A long sandbank.

SEAMS 86 The lines where planks joined on the outside of a ship. The seams were stuffed with old rope or cloth and covered in tar to stop water leaking in.

SECOND MATE 29 A ship's officer under the captain and *first mate*.

SERVING MALLET 73

SETTING SAILS 21

SHEET ANCHOR 84

SHIP'S BISCUITS 20

SHIP'S LOG 51 A book that was used to record where and how far a ship had travelled.

SHORTENING SAIL 33, 79 Reducing the amount of sail hanging from the *yards*.

SKIFF 30 See also *boats*.

SLAVER 74 A person who trades slaves.

SMUGGLING 18, 99

SPAR 13

SPLICING AND COVERING 73

STARBOARD 15

STAYS 85

STEM 15

STERN 15

STOCKADE 57 A barrier made of wooden stakes.

STORM 68, 79–85, 96

SUPERSTITION 29, 50, 69

SURGERY 42

SWEEPS 74

Sources

Writers and illustrators owe a debt of gratitude to the authors and artists whose works inspire them. Richard Platt and Chris Riddell are especially grateful, because they searched in more than forty books for details that would make the text and pictures of *Pirate Diary* authentic. There isn't room here to list them all, but the following were among the more useful books.

Bayliss, A.E.M.: **Dampier's Voyages**

Botting, Douglas: **The Pirates**

Chapelle, Howard I.: **The History of American Sailing Ships**

Cordingly, David: **Life Among the Pirates**

Cordingly, David (ed.): **Pirates**

Cordingly, David, & Falconer, John: **Pirates, Fact and Fiction**

Esquemeling, John: **Buccaneers of America**

Hall, Daniel Weston: **Arctic Rovings, or the Adventures of a New Bedford Boy on Sea and Land**

Johnson, Charles: **Lives of the Most Notorious Pirates**

Kemp, Peter (ed.): **Oxford Companion to Ships and the Sea**

Mitchell, David: **Pirates**

Rodger, N.A.M.: **The Wooden World**

Stone, William T., & Hays, Ann M.: **A Cruising Guide to the Caribbean**

Willoughby, Captain R.M.: **Square Rig Seamanship**

Inspiration also came from **Howard Pyle**, whose outstanding pirate illustrations helped fire the imaginations of countless people.

Thanks are due to all of the people who helped and advised the author, illustrator and publisher on this project; in particular: **David D. Moore** at the **North Carolina Maritime Museum**, in Beaufort, USA; the staff of **The National Maritime Museum** in Greenwich, London; **Alison Toplis**; **David Cordingly**; **David** and **Kristina Torr**; and **Ken Kinkor** and **Barry Clifford** of **Expedition Whydah**.

FLIP-OVER CASTLE

AND READ
DIARY

CASTLE DIARY

Sent to his uncle's castle to learn to be a page,
eleven-year-old Toby keeps a detailed diary
of everything that happens there during the
year of 1285 – from boar hunts and tournaments to
baking bread and cleaning out toilets!

"Accessible history, full of accurate detail ...
unadulterated fun to read." *The Guardian*

"A must for budding historians."
The Independent on Sunday

Shortlisted for the *Kurt Maschler Award*,
the *TES Junior Information Book Award*,
the *New Generation History Book of the Year Prize*
and Highly Commended for the
Kate Greenaway Medal

For Joan Clayton, who despite her best efforts
failed to turn her son into a pageboy
R.P.

For William
C.R.

First published 1999 by Walker Books Ltd
87 Vauxhall Walk, London SE11 5HJ

This edition published for Ottakar's 2005

2 4 6 8 10 9 7 5 3 1

Text © 1999 Richard Platt
Illustrations © 1999 Chris Riddell

The right of Richard Platt and Chris Riddell to be identified respectively as the author
and illustrator of this work has been asserted by them in accordance with the
Copyright, Designs and Patents Act 1988

This book has been typeset in Truesdell and Francesca

Printed and bound in Great Britain by Creative Print and Design (Wales), Ebbw Vale

British Library Cataloguing in Publication Data:
a catalogue record for this book
is available from the British Library

ISBN 0-7445-7025-5

www.walkerbooks.co.uk

CASTLE DIARY

The Journal of
Tobias Burgess, Page

RICHARD PLATT

illuminated by CHRIS RIDDELL

OTTAKAR'S

Strandborough Castle

1 Drawbridge
2 Moat
3 Gatehouse and Guardrooms
4 Bailey
5 Keep
6 Great Hall
7 Great Chamber (Solar)
8 Toby's Room
9 Chapel
10 Kitchens
11 Kitchen Garden
12 Aunt Elizabeth's Garden
13 Stables and Armoury
14 Kennels
15 Archery Butts
16 North Wall
17 Little Wood
18 Mill
19 Well

This Journal, being the diary of myself, Tobias Burgess, begins this day, the 2nd of January, in the year of Our Lord, 1285.

I write these words at my home in the parish of Saltington. Here I dwell with my father Henry, my mother Gwynedd, and my two younger sisters Edythe and Sian.

But soon I shall be leaving here, for I am to spend the next twelvemonth (and more, I hope) as a page at the castle of my father's elder brother, John Burgess, Baron of Strandborough.

My uncle has expected me these past two years, but my mother wept and would not let me go. In just two days, though, I shall be eleven years of age, and my father says I can wait no longer. At last I am to be taught the

skills and duties I must know to become a squire and even, mayhap, a knight – if my father can afford it!

My mother bids me write this journal so that I will remember all that passes, and can tell her of it when I see her next. For though Strandborough Castle is not twenty miles distant, 'tis most difficult country to cross and, as few people journey that way, news from there is scarce.

Now all that stops me is the weather, for the snow lies so thickly on the ground that the roads can barely be seen, let alone travelled upon! The delay tries both my patience and that of Hugh, my father's servant, whose task it is to deliver me to Strandborough. Though I shall be sad to leave my family (except for my sister Sian, who vexes me daily), I scarce can wait to begin my new life.

January 10th, Wednesday

Our arrival made me feel most grand, for when we were yet some distance away the watchman did spy us out and sound his horn, and my cousin Simon rode out to greet

us. Simon is full-grown and soon to be a knight, but I was greatly pleased to see him as he was kind to me when last he visited my father.

We entered the castle through a great gateway and into the Bailey beyond – my father's manor house, and his stables, would fit easily in this huge courtyard.

At the far end stands a strong tower house called the Keep. Within the Keep is the Great Hall, which is used for eating and other gatherings. The family live in newer dwellings built against the South Wall. Here Simon showed me where I would sleep and left me. I am to share my room with three other pages. We sleep on wooden pallets with mattresses of straw, like at home.

I confess I am so tired from the journey that I barely have strength to write these words.

January 11th, Thursday

I awoke this morning early and had chance to observe the other pages while they slept. The one who woke next shared some bread with me. He told me his name was Mark and asked me mine. As we ate he pointed at the other sleeping pages, and laughed: "See Toby – Oliver and Humphrey shall have no bread, for they slumber still."

Soon Simon came to take me to the Great Hall, where my Aunt Elizabeth sat by a huge fire. She welcomed me fondly and told me that my uncle attends the King in the west of the country, but will return in a few days.

Then my aunt bade me greet my other cousins, Simon's sisters, Abigail and Beth. Abigail, who is the fairer of face, is younger than I, and her sister is older. When we were introduced Abigail blushed and looked at me from the tail of her eye. "Toby is here to learn the duties of a page," my aunt told them, "but this day I would like you to show him our home." Then, turning to me, she added that on the morrow I would learn what I must do to make myself useful.

January 12th, Friday

I find that everyone calls my uncle and aunt "My Lord" and "My Lady", and that I must do likewise. There are so many strange things to learn and do here that today I have time to write only a line or two. I fear my journal will have many gaps in it!

January 13th, Saturday

Directly after we had broken our fast yesterday, my aunt summoned me and spoke to me of my duties. Pages here serve my aunt and uncle, and thus learn courtesy, and the manners and customs of a noble family.

Like the other pages, I am expected to make myself useful by running errands and carrying messages and suchlike. At mealtimes I will learn to serve my aunt and uncle and their guests – to fill their cups, and carve them slices of meat which I will place before them in a genteel way.

But as I am her nephew, I am also to be my aunt's

personal page and
must hold myself
ready at all times
to attend her.
(Though
I thought
this an honour,
Humphrey – who is
the oldest of the pages here – scorned
it, saying my aunt will have a sharper eye than most for
my errors.)

Much of this seemed to me to be dull stuff, so I asked
my aunt if I might also ride in a hunt. She did not
answer, but instead told me of my studies. The castle
Chaplain is away at present, for he visits with the Bishop,
but on his return I will join the other pages under his
tutelage. With this, my aunt bade me make myself
familiar with the many buildings and places within the
castle walls, and then dismissed me.

January 14th, The Lord's Day

This noon 'twas my task to serve my aunt at table, though I fear that through the nervous shaking of my hand as much food fell to the floor as was placed before her.

The Hall was crowded, for there are many servants here, and it will be some days before I will properly know one from t'other. Only two of them are women, and one is constantly at my aunt's side. This woman, whose name is Isbel, dresses finely in clothes quite like my aunt's. The other is Isbel's maid. She wears clothes of red and blue, the same colours as the uniforms of many of the men servants.

I found it very odd that my aunt's servant should herself have a servant. But when I asked my aunt to explain she answered me sharply, saying, "Watch your tongue! Though she does my bidding, Isbel is no peasant girl. She is as much my companion as my servant. Like you, and many others who serve your uncle and me, she comes from a good family and is used to soft clothes and

being waited upon." Then my aunt said, "Why, even a servant's servants sometimes need servants!"

And 'twas true, as I soon discovered. The Steward, for instance, who seems a prim and fussy man, is the most senior of the servants and is in charge of I know not how many others. Among those he instructs is the Butler, whose duty it is to care for the castle wines and ales. The Butler in turn commands the Cellarer, who stores the wine. And even the Cellarer has boys to lift the barrels for him.

All but the lowest servants eat together in the Hall, and we pages sit with them when our serving duties are done.

January 15th, Monday

I attended my aunt today in the Great Chamber. This is where my aunt and uncle sleep, but by day my aunt receives visitors there and instructs the servants in the running of the castle. At home we call this room the Solar, though ours is smaller by far. My aunt is always busy, for it is she who directs the Steward in the management of the castle household. She jokes that when my uncle is away she must do all her own work and also everything he does – except for shaving!

January 16th, Tuesday

With my aunt again this day and met more of the people who aid her in her daily busy-ness. Within the walls, it is the Constable who minds the castle when my aunt and uncle are both away at their other estates. When my aunt told him who I was he did not smile or speak, but sighed deeply as if I had already wronged him.

With him also was the Reeve. This man has charge of

all the manor – the farms and forest and common lands belonging to the castle. The Reeve collects the rents and taxes which those who dwell on the manor must pay to my uncle regularly for their housing and farms – and for other privileges such as the right to collect firewood in the forest.

January 17th, Wednesday

Today returned my uncle. When I was summoned to greet him, he clapped me firmly on the shoulder and told me that I would make a fine page.

I asked him if I could have a horse (much missing my own pony, which Hugh had taken home) and when I could ride in a hunt. But he laughed and said only: "Patience lad, thou shalt learn of such things in time."

My uncle says I am to study archery, and mayhap fighting with a sword, for I shall need these noble skills when I become a squire and learn the craft of knighthood. Knights serve the King and do battle against

his foes. But they must be honourable as well as brave, so squires also study the rules of chivalry – which means doing noble deeds and helping and respecting everyone.

January 20th, Saturday

This day returned the Chaplain to lead our daily worship. He it is who has the task of teaching us pages, as well as writing letters for my aunt when she is busy with her other duties. Now not only must we rise an hour earlier each morn to attend Mass, but schooling will begin again soon!

January 22nd, Monday

This day I spent in schooling with the other pages and with my cousins Abigail and Beth. If we have no other duties, we start our studies after Mass and breaking fast, and continue as long as there is daylight enough to read by.

Chaplain teaches us Latin and the Scriptures. We also study our letters with him, and our numbers. My mother has taught me well in reading and writing in English and

I am ahead of most (excepting Beth, who is most studious for a girl), but Latin is new to me, and I must learn many pages of the most dull books.

January 23rd, Tuesday

Studying today was no better than yesterday. It seems that most of my days will be taken up like this until my fourteenth birthday. Then I shall become a squire (if I do not die from boredom first). Mark whispered to me that all schooling, everywhere, is like this. The Chaplain, seeing us speak, did thrash me, but I did not cry out. Later, Mark warned me that Chaplain beats us more in winter. "'Tis surely because the room is cold, and whipping warms both his arms and our rumps," said Mark!

January 24th, Wednesday

This forenoon a squire fetched me during our Latin studies. He said that my uncle has commanded a HUNT for Saturday, and I should make haste to the stables to try out the horse they had for me!

My heart leaped at this. At home, Mother forbids me to ride with hounds (even though Father would allow it), for she fears I shall fall.

The stables lie along the North Wall, and are grander and in better repair than many cottages I have seen. Here they keep many different kinds of horses, for sport and for work, and they look less hungry, too, than the people who labour in the fields, and are certainly cleaner.

The man who has charge of the stables is called the "Sergeant-Farrier", and such is his skill, Mark tells me, that many outside the castle seek his advice when their horses fall sick.

The greatest of the horses are two huge warhorses, called destriers, that my uncle rides in battle. There are

also three lesser horses, called palfreys, that he uses when he is not riding in the King's service. Then there are coursers for hunting, gentle hackneys for ladies to ride and great numbers of packhorses and carthorses.

Sergeant-Farrier brought me Prancer, who is a courser. She is a fine horse, bigger and much better bred than my nag Hobby at home. He led me out into the Bailey. Then, seeing I could handle her, he let me ride out through the gatehouse and across the meadows beyond.

Prancer is much faster than Hobby, too, and in my excitement I did not notice that my hat had taken flight from my head. When I had retrieved it, I galloped on across the fields and tried to imagine myself leading the chase!

January 25th, Thursday

Humphrey and Oliver made great sport last night about my horse and the hunt. They pretend they have no wish to "tear their clothes and muddy themselves in the

destrier

courser

hackney

palfrey

packhorse

forest". But they make fun of me because in truth they too wish to hunt, and I am promised this adventure only because I am my uncle's nephew.

January 26th, Friday

Was teased without mercy again today, but this time by Mark because (he says) while sleeping I did gallop as if my bed were a horse, and woke them all by shouting "HOO STO!" and other such hunting calls.

For lateness at school Mark was punished with the finger pillory. I laughed, and for this had to join him. Chaplain made us stand one hour with our fingers held tight between the pillory's boards.

I fear I shall sleep as little as a cat this night. For my mind spins with thoughts of the morrow's venture. I pray that it will be a success.

January 27th, Saturday

The baying of hounds woke me before dawn this day, and I opened the shutter just in time to see the kennel-lads fixing bells around the dogs' necks, which I thought most odd.

Breakfast was a much grander affair than the bread and ale that we usually enjoy, for gathered with my uncle in the Hall were many other noble folk from neighbouring manors.

The talk was all of THE HUNT. It seems that my uncle's manor is a better place than most for such sport. He and his squires hunt deer or hare or fox each week at least, though rarely with so many noble friends. Today, though, we were to hunt BOAR, which is the most exciting and dangerous of all quarry. (This, I learned, is why the dogs wear bells – the noise of them scares the

beast, which otherwise is so fierce it will kill half the pack!)

At last the signal was given and the hunt set off. We rode from the castle to the forest's edge before releasing the hounds. But then, though I followed as fast as I dared, I was soon left far behind.

Ahead of me I could hear the hounds baying with great excitement, and I guessed they had found a boar. Then I heard the Huntsman signal the end of the chase with a long note on his horn, and I knew I had missed the best moment.

The tracks of the
horses led me to a clearing
where the Huntsman had already
cut open the beast and given its guts to
the dogs. A squire I did not know told me the
boar had fought bravely, turning at the end to face
the pack. But the hounds had kept the boar at bay until the
huntsmen could surround it and kill it with spears and
swords. I was sore dismayed not to have seen such a sight.

What's more, I lost my way on the journey back to the
castle. 'Twas dusk before I returned, and now I have had no
supper!

February 5th, Monday

Chaplain sickened this forenoon and took to his bed, so we were free to do as we pleased. To help me forget my misery over the hunt (and because he was sick of hearing me tell of it), Mark offered to teach me longshanks – this being his name for stilts.

He led me to the old sally port in the West Wall. This small door was once a back way out of the castle but is scarce used today.

We went to the little wood that grows beyond the wall and there Mark showed me how to cut a forked chestnut branch, with one side long to hold on to, and the other short to stand on. I soon discovered that my stilts were far more easily made than used, though, and have bruises aplenty to show for it!

February 6th, Tuesday

Back to schooling this day. Sitting in the cold Keep fair freezed me to the bone, so when lessons were ended I slipped into the kitchen. While thawing in its warmth I watched a kitchen-lad making pie shells, which he did call coffins.

Not many minutes had passed before the Cook espied me heating myself by the bread oven. He asked my business there and when he learned that I had no task said, "There is no room in my kitchen for useless bodies," and set me to copying from a pile of recipes that he had. They were much splattered and a few even smelled of the dishes they described. Some were most strange, especially a salad made with cocks' combs and hens' feet. For writing on, Cook gave me some old scraps of parchment. Many had to be scraped clean before I could use them again.

February 13th, Tuesday

Before lessons I went again to warm myself in the kitchen and watched while Cook made bread. He and his helpers start work before dawn, and the kitchen was a busy, bustling place. Cook mixes water and flour with barm. This last stuff he gets from the Brewess in the village, who calls it yeast. Her work is to make ale for the castle, and as it brews she scoops off the barm that floats on the top as foam. This barm forms bubbles that swell the dough, making the bread light. Cook kneads the dough in a trough made of the hollowed-out half of a tree-trunk, then shapes it into loaves and leaves it to rise.

February 14th, Wednesday

Cook showed me today how they bake bread. A kitchen-lad lights the oven early on baking days, so that it is hot when the loaves are ready for baking.

He begins by burning bundles of sticks and then throws in a log or two. As soon as the oven glows over

all, he scoops out the embers, brushes out most of the grey ash, then wipes the oven floor with a wet mop. The oven hisses mightily, and steam issues from its mouth like the breath of a dragon.

Cook then sets the loaves into the hot oven with a wooden shovel he calls a peel.

They bake here three kinds of bread. Cook made me miniature loaves of each sort and all the kitchen staff rested at their work to watch me taste them. The best, called manchet, is made from sifted wheaten flour and is the white bread we eat in Hall. The second, brown cheat bread, I knew also, for I have seen some of the servants eat it.

The last, which I did not know, they call brom-bread. It was horrible and I spat it out, which caused great mirth among those who watched.

I learned later that only dogs and horses eat such bread. It is baked to use up the bran the miller sieves out from the wheat when he makes white flour. At such ill-use I ran out of the kitchen and vowed not to go back there even if the ice freezes off all my fingers!

February 21st, Wednesday

Tomorrow I am to spend the day at the butts (which is what they call the archery targets here), and must do so in the company of the Constable. Part of his work as warden of the castle is to train the castle guards and ensure that they are constantly ready to ward off an attack. To this end, he and his men practise their fighting skills as often as the weather and their other duties will allow.

To him also is given the task of instructing us pages in the basic points of archery, though clearly he does not relish such a chore, for when my uncle asked him to watch over me at the butts he protested loudly. He said that I was old enough to look after myself (which is true).

But my uncle silenced him, saying, "Hush man, 'tis just for one day! Once he has the hang of it he can practise without your help. But this is my brother's only son. What say he if the lad be spiked with an arrow on his first day at yonder butts?"

February 22nd, Thursday

This morn the Constable and I ventured out together to the butts beyond the North Wall (each of us pretending that we were alone).

At home I have a bow which Father fashioned for me, but when I saw what they call here a "boy's bow", I knew mine was but a toy.

My new bow is made of yew wood, and is as tall as me. Straight as an iron rod, it is almost as stiff. To bend it and fit the string takes all my strength.

My arrows are the perfect twins of those the castle guards use, but done in miniature. They have real goose-feather flights, which are supposed to make them fly straight at the target.

Oftener, though, my arrows fly elsewhere when I let go the bow string. I had thought that my practice with arrows in the orchard at home last summer might be some help to me in this new endeavour, but I am by far the poorest archer in the castle!

March 3rd, Saturday

Have been neglectful of my journal of late, for studies and other tasks fill the daylight hours when it is light enough to write. I made this entry in school while I did pretend to be studying my numbers.

At the butts yesterday one of the archers showed me why his kind are so feared by our King's foes. With bow in hand he stood before a tree with a trunk thicker than my chest. He pulled back the bow string until the veins stood out upon his face, and when he loosed the arrow its head passed clean through the tree-trunk and pierced the other side.

Seeing this, the other archers jeered that he was showing off, and four more of them repeated his trick. But then when he let fly thirteen arrows in a minute none took up his challenge to better him.

March 9th, Friday

Practised archery again today. This time I was much

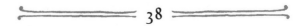

better and pulled the
string right back. But
when the Constable
saw this he gave me a
bigger bow, so once
again I am the castle
dizzard at the butts.

Of twelve arrows
I shot with my new bow, only four hit
target, while seven fell on grass. One killed a sparrow in
flight. Those watching cried "HAIL!" and clapped, so
I bowed low to them and said not that 'twas but a fluke.

March 11th, The Lord's Day

With much ceremony a special dish was placed before
me at dinner today. Baked on a skewer was the bird that
I had shot. Cook, whose jest this was, called it "Sparrow
à l'Arrow". And though there was scarce a mouthful of
meat on the bird, it tasted well.

March 12th, Monday

This morn I overheard my uncle say he was to visit the castle armoury to see about some small changes to his helm. He wishes it to weigh less heavy on his head, yet better protect him at the JOUSTS!

Of this tournament I knew nothing and I begged his leave to accompany him. In my excitement I quite forgot myself and began to say, "Uncle, tell me more about...", for I desired most keenly to learn of these jousts. But then I remembered my manners, and blushing began anew: "My Lord, if it pleases you, pray tell me more about the tournament."

This made him laugh, and he spoke freely about it, saying that the jousts are to be held, as usual, on Saint George's feast day. So I must wait SIX WEEKS!

Within the armoury they make and mend all manner of weapons as well as armour. But the noise of hammering and the heat from the furnace in which they soften the metal were so great that they made my head whirl.

'Tis certain the sound has made the Armourer and the Smith and their apprentices as deaf as beetles, for to make himself heard my uncle had to bellow like a braying ass.

March 16th, Friday

My cousin Beth hath sewed me a shirt of Egyptiacal cotton! I have never before had such dainty garb. I hastened to put it on, but because it is new the seams and stitches rubbed my skin sore.

Humphrey and Oliver both laughed at this and called me "chrisomer" and "nigget" and "moonling". They are accustomed to new clothes and will suffer them until washing softens the folds. But I would rather wear my old linen shirt, for though it is more common, 'tis also more comfortable.

March 19th, Monday

Played at knights with Mark, Oliver and Humphrey today. As Mark is bigger than me, he was the horse and I rode his back. We won. Oliver toppled from his horse and got a bloody nose. Serves him right, for he did twist my ears most painfully and call me the worst names when first I wore my new shirt.

March 20th, Tuesday

Wrote yesternight by candle's flicker and fell asleep with quill in hand. When I awoke, the candle had set the pages alight, and would have burned my straw mattress or worse if Humphrey had not smelled smoke and beat out the flames. This morning Chaplain likewise beat my backside – to teach me care with candles, he said.

Ate salt fish again today. DISGUSTING! Here they are more careful to follow the Church's rules than at home, so besides every Tuesday, Friday and Saturday being fish days, they also eat fish on each Church festival. This means we eat vile fish more often than flesh or fowl.

April 11th, Wednesday

Watched my uncle practise for the jousts today. He charged eleven times at a wooden ring hung from a tree, and caught it on his lance five times. It takes much skill to lift the ring from its hook while galloping at full speed, and all who saw this agree it bodes well for the contest.

April 22nd, The Lord's Day

Tomorrow begin the jousts! The host of noble knights who accepted my uncle's challenge are lodged at inns nearby, or are encamped upon the fields outside the castle.

TWO-SCORE gaily coloured tents sprouted in the night like mushrooms. Flying from lances planted in the ground, the knights' pennants look like flowers in a spring meadow.

All the talk is of who shall prevail, and methinks the men of the castle guard place wagers on the winner. I pray my uncle shall vanquish them all!

April 23rd, Monday

This being the feast day of Saint George, the whole castle was astir well before sunrise in preparation for the jousts.

All the clashes were keenly fought, but I shall give account of my uncle's combat first. His opponent was Lord Sudbury. Everyone from the castle (and the village folk besides) gathered eagerly to watch their charge.

After some ceremony, of which I shall tell later, the two knights trotted to opposite ends of the Lists (which is what they call the strip of field where the combat takes place). When they were some 300 paces apart they

turned to face each other.

The sunlight danced on their shiny helms, and on the bright colours of their families' arms blazoned on their shields and armour.

On the command "LAISSEZ ALLER" from a herald, both knights urged their horses forward. Pricked with sharp spurs, the snorting horses galloped faster and faster, until they ran as swift as a March gale. Each knight aimed his lance at the shield of the other, and the watchers cried "HUZZAH!" when my uncle stayed on his horse and knocked Sudbury to the ground. Three times my uncle toppled Sudbury.

At their third meeting, though, the force of Sudbury's blow lifted my uncle, too, clean from his saddle.

Those who watched gasped "ALAS!" in fear for my uncle's life, but he quickly rose to his feet and raised his iron glove to still the hubbub.

Then, though, he found that he could not raise the visor on his helm, so twisted it was from the fall. And when later the heralds announced that my uncle was the victor, he was nowhere to be found.

At length, a search of the castle discovered my uncle in the armoury – with his head laid on an anvil and the Smith at work upon his helm. 'Tis surely a wonder the Smith could remove it without harming a hair of my uncle's head.

April 25th, Wednesday

There seems each day of the jousts to be less sport than the day before, and more boring ceremony. Before combat begins each morn, the knights withdraw to their arming tents where squires help them dress for the jousts. When they return, fully armed, there is much bowing low and making of speeches. When these dull preparations are complete, the heralds proclaim the names of the combatants, whose faces are hidden behind their shiny helms.

Only then do the first two knights face each other and spur their horses on, and to my mind the excitement that follows is over far too soon.

April 26th, Thursday

The jousting ends at last! I swear I should die of boredom if I were to listen to just one more speech. And after so many charges all knights look the same. If I had known it would be thus, I should have feigned illness on Monday and so escaped the ordeal.

The new hose that I wear for this grand event is hot, for it clings to my legs as tightly as the skin clings to a sausage. And it is my duty to wait upon my aunt all day while she watches, which tires me much.

Gilbert, Earl of Hertford, was this day mortally wounded in the jousts. But when I talked of it with Mark he only said: "Well, 'tis common."

May 3rd, Thursday

Today was an Egypty day. And as all know, ill fortune follows any work that starts on these two unlucky days in the month. Our Chaplain cautioned us that 'twas but a superstition from heathen Egypt. My uncle also told us we should not mind it. Later, though, I heard him tell a groom to put away the horses he had saddled, for only fools start journeys on Egypty days.

May 14th, Monday

While we studied this forenoon my cousin Abigail

scratched a message in her wax tablet and passed it to me. Chaplain seized it and now I must rise before dawn for a week and pray with him. This seems to me most UNJUST! I am punished, though I did no wrong. She did wrong, yet is not punished.

(May 27th, The Lord's Day

Yesterday was one of great celebration, for my uncle dubbed Simon a knight. Now he is twenty-one, Simon has been full seven years a squire and has learned well the noble skills of knighthood.

Two days did Simon spend in prayer and fasting. On Friday night he slept not at all, but kept vigil in the Chapel, praying until dawn. Then, at cock-crow, he bathed and dressed in a tunic of pure white, and attended Mass. Only after this could he break his fast and venture out into the Bailey for the armouring ceremony.

First, my uncle dressed him in a coat of mail. Then Simon put on a gleaming helm and gilded spurs, and

grasped a shield painted with the two Burgess ravens. When this was done he knelt to await the colee – the blow from my uncle's sword that would make him a knight.

I thought this would be no more than a light tap, and was alarmed to see how heavy was the blow. But Simon was expecting it thus. He rose speedily, and swore a solemn vow to be a gallant and brave knight. Then all cheered as he mounted a fine Spanish palfrey and rode round the Bailey. Later, there was feasting in the Hall in

Simon's honour. He will make a fine knight; and he is a good and kind cousin.

June 9th, Saturday

The weather of late has been fearsome hot. We have not seen a cloud in weeks, and the ground is parched from want of rain. The river has sunk lower than any can remember, and green SLIME grows in that part of the moat where we usually swim.

In the Bailey two men dig a new well. This is oft a wet and muddy task, but as there is little water to fill the well the men can work dry-foot.

June 13th, Wednesday

The garderobes all reek. When I have need of them I rush in nimbly, clutching my nose. I let fall my hose and pray that relief will be quick. This forenoon when I sat upon the wooden seat, out from under it flew a black fly so fat that at first I took it to be a wren.

June 15th, Friday

This day the GONG-FARMER came from
the village to work below the South Wall.
On this side of the castle the garderobes empty
down chutes into the moat. But because there
has been no rain, the moat is sluggish in its
flow and everything that falls from the chutes
stays where it drops. The Gong-Farmer must
clear not only these piles but others besides,
for elsewhere in the castle the garderobes
empty into pits, which must be cleaned to
keep them sweet.

One of the garderobe chutes is blocked
and the Gong-Farmer must reach up inside
this slimy pipe to unclog it. I would not
do his job for all the King's gold.

A humming black cloud hangs
always above a Gong-
Farmer's head. Nose

warns of his approach long before eyes espy him, and all ears are alert to the squeaking of his stinking cart.

June 20th, Wednesday

Woke two nights past to the crashing of thunder. Now the rain does not stop and we are awash with water!

July 9th, Monday

Today at table my aunt and uncle talked softly mouth to ear. Isbel, my aunt's companion, has told me that a grand earl is coming to Strandborough. He and his household are journeying north and will rest at the castle for at least two nights. I divined from their talk that my aunt and uncle are already planning a great banquet for the visit, even though 'tis still some weeks away.

July 14th, Saturday

This morn my aunt told Isbel the reason for my uncle's keen preparations, and as she is friendly towards me Isbel

has entrusted me also with the secret. It seems this great Earl has the ear of the King, and my uncle hopes to gain favour by welcoming him. Though my uncle's castle is grand, this Earl has an estate many times larger. As there are pebbles on a beach, so he has gold coins in equal numbers.

July 20th, Friday

Isbel tutored me in table manners this day (though I needed it not). "If you eat with the Earl's household while they are here," said she, "have a care to spit politely on the floor, not over the table."

When I sniffed, she reminded me that if I should wipe my nose, it is only seemly to clean my hand on my clothes before touching food.

July 27th, Friday

Towards the end of lessons today we heard music from beyond the castle walls. Abigail and I made haste to find out whence had come this sound, and Simon told us that

a band of players had passed by on their way to the village inn. They have come at my uncle's bidding for the banquet. These folk journey near and far, singing for their bread, and Simon has said he will take us to see them on the morrow.

July 28th, Saturday

We found the players outside the village church, amusing a crowd of folk. The tumblers were most marvellous and though one showed me how he walks on his hands, I could not master even one step.

The minstrels sang of our King's victory in the west. Their verses brought news, too, of wars and great happenings in other lands. Most songs were jolly, though, and the crowd that was gathered there knew them of old and joined in with the choruses.

A few folk dropped a farthing in a leathern hat which the tumblers passed around. Others gave them bread or cheese, or brought a jug of ale to pay for this fine entertainment.

July 30th, Monday

Today, two great ox-carts trundled across the drawbridge to the kitchen yard. It took Cook's servants near half the day to unload and store all the provisions. The first cart bore barrels of wine and ale so large they had to be rolled, for they could not be lifted. The second cart held all manner of meats and fish. One was most strange, with the tail of a fish but the fur of a beast and the face of a man with whiskers complete. Later, Cook told me 'twas some kind of sea beast. 'Tis fantastical food we shall be eating when at last we sit down at our trenchers!

On Wednesday arrives the Earl, and on Thursday will be the banquet.

August 7th, Tuesday

These five days past the whole household supped in Hall in honour of our most noble guest, the Earl of Branstone.

But straightway after the feast a fever afflicted me and I was taken to lie in the Great Chamber, where my aunt

and Isbel could watch over me. Though somewhat
recovered, I am as weak as a kitten and must stay in bed –
so shall use the time to write of past events, for I fear I
neglect my journal. The feast itself was the grandest thing
I have ever seen. I could not help but stare at the many fine
clothes and the gold and silver dishes.

It was the food, though, that caused all
present to gasp in amazement and
marvel at the seemingly endless
array of dishes. Here were
majestic peacocks, stuffed
and roasted and proudly
dressed in their feathers,
and there the tiny tongues
of larks. And fish of all
kinds in plenty, baked and
boiled, and platter after
platter of roasted meats
rich with sauces.

The Earl had come with a host of servants who helped us bring out the dishes for each course. Each dish was carried in with much ceremony and presented to my uncle and the Earl before it was served. When the dishes were laid on the tables we sat down to eat.

There were a great many dishes I did not recognize. One seemed half bird, half beast. Mark named it: "Cockatrice, 'tis called, but I know not where it is hunted." This made Humphrey laugh so hard that he almost spat out his food. "Mark!" he snorted. "'Tis but a kitchen trick. First they pluck a big fowl and cut it across the waist. Then they take a piglet, likewise cut in half, and sew top of one to bottom of t'other."

This cockatrice tasted good, but the noble Earl would not eat of it (or of any other dish) before his butler had tasted it to see if it was fit for his master.

I tire now, and so shall write more upon the morrow.

August 8th, Wednesday

I have told how grandly we ate at the feast. But in a few ways this banquet was like ordinary fare. As usual, of course, we ate with knife, spoon and fingers and heaped our food upon trenchers of hard, stale cheat bread cut into thick slices.

Drink, too, was much the same. But instead of the weak penny ale that is all we pages are normally allowed, the cup-bearers poured us twopenny ale, which tasted far stronger.

As it grew later the ale loosened everyone's tongues, and Humphrey and Oliver began to make rude fun of me. When I sat with my legs apart, Oliver did point to where they joined beneath my thin hose. With much glee he chanted: "Let not thy privy members be laid open to be viewed. 'Tis most shameful and abhorred, detestable and rude!"

The tail of this rhyme I scarcely heard, for just then the minstrels blew a fanfare. Both they and the tumblers

had been entertaining us all most skilfully (though some of the minstrels' songs were saucy and made the ladies blush and bashfully study the floor).

The horns that drowned Oliver's words announced a subtlety. The subtleties were cunningly fashioned from sugar and almond paste and were one of the delicacies that ended each of the four courses.

They were goodly sweet to taste, though they did not look like food at all. One was modelled as a hunting scene, and another as a mythic beast. But my favourite was one that looked like a great ship tossed at sea.

After the fanfare I remember no more, for this was when (or so I am told) I sickened and fell headlong to the floor.

August 9th, Thursday

Because I am still weak and do not mend as quickly as my aunt would wish, my uncle has sent Simon to fetch a physician from Middlethorpe.

This town is but an hour's ride from Strandborough, though my uncle said that as he doubts I am dying, Simon need not rush to return before tomorrow.

August 10th, Friday

The Physician arrived today. Leach he is called and the name describes him well, for he is round and sleek and I like him not!

First he had me relieve myself into a glass flask so he could study my water. He held it up to the window to judge the colour, and then brought it to his nose. I guessed he would drink from it next, but instead he set it down on the table. Then he took from his purse a folded piece of parchment and, opening it, studied its mysterious signs and marks with great care.

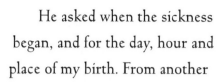

He asked when the sickness
began, and for the day, hour and
place of my birth. From another
chart he worked out how
stood the stars when I
sickened (for this also affects
his choice of cure). Then he
announced: "The boy is
melancholic, and Earth fights Fire
for control of his body." This surprised me
not a little, for I had thought it was the surfeit of food
and ale I had swallowed at the banquet that ailed my gut.

Finally he added that I should be bled, but as this was
not a favourable time for such a task he would return, if
needed, in a few days.

August 12th, The Lord's Day

Still I am confined to my bed in the Great Chamber.
When I tried to rise this morn, the room swung so

wildly about me that I felt sick to my stomach again and my aunt straightway made me lie back down.

Today my aunt received a visitor. This woman, who is called Lady Cecily, is my aunt's friend and lives in the neighbouring manor of Littlethorpe. She brought with her a younger sister, Jane. Together the four women wiled away the day in working at their needlepoint and playing chess and backgammon. Mostly, though, they gossiped of the banquet and of the noble knights they knew. Later, Jane and Isbel tried to teach me backgammon, but my brain was too muddled to make much sense of it.

When they went to eat in the Hall, Mark sneaked in to see how I did, which cheered me greatly.

August 13th, Monday

Doctor Leach came again today, and after much peering and prodding he declared once more that I must be bled to release the ill humours or fluids that are in my body.

Grasping hold of my arm, he straightway chose a vein and opened it with a knife. He told my aunt that this would let out the black bile, of which I have too much. And that as the moon is nearly full, this is a good time for bloodletting.

At length the Leach bandaged up my arm and taking out a piece of parchment wrote the letters of my name on it. Then he gave each of the letters a number, summed them all together, and announced: "The boy shall live!"

At this my aunt near swooned with joy, and paid the fat Doctor well for his work. But I feel sicker than ever and my arm hurts abominably.

August 16th, Thursday

Today I am much mended, though my arm still pains me not a little. I cannot think how bleeding someone helps to cure them. 'Tis my belief I am recovered in spite of Doctor Leach's treatment rather than because of it.

August 24th, Friday

Though I am now full recovered, I did this morn feign illness. The day was bright and clear, and after so much time indoors I had no heart for spending more in dull schooling.

While my cousins and the other pages were at their studies, I slipped out and walked along the river bank towards the forest.

The corn stands high and yellow in the fields, for reaping will soon begin. At first I saw no one, and had only the skylarks and rabbits for company. But then I spied some sudden movement in the distance and, being curious, made haste to find out what it was.

When I drew closer I spied a man lying on the river bank. He was now perfectly still, gazing into the water. His hand was in the water, too, and near it a fish stirred.

The fish swam right up to the man and over his hand. Suddenly the silence ended, and all was splashing as the man hurled the flapping fish on to the bank.

The poacher (for such I guessed he was) sprang to his feet and then saw me. He looked at me and I at him. We two looked at the fish, which thrashed on the grass. He stooped and picked up the wriggling fish and, swinging it by the tail, brought its head down on a tree-stump.

The fish went still, and he laid it down next to another one.

"Thou hast not seen me, hast thou boy?" he growled. I did not understand him and said nothing. At this he swore beneath his breath and raised his fist. "Thou hast not seen me, nor the fish!"

I turned, but before I could run his hand shot out and grabbed my arm. Then he knelt down, and bringing his

face close to mine began to talk more calmly.

"Now lad, thou shouldst not be here, shouldst thou?" he questioned.

He smelled of onions and ale, and though his voice was soft his grip was not, so I confessed it was the truth.

"Well then," he said, "you keep us meeting here a secret and so shall I. Agreed?"

I wished he would let go my arm, so promised I'd say nothing. When his grip slackened I burst free and hurried back to the castle.

August 26th, The Lord's Day

This coming week the harvesting begins and the castle corn will be cut. I pleaded with my aunt to let me go into the fields and help, as I do at home.

She said at first 'twas not right for a boy of my good birth to work in the fields. But seeing that I craved it she did bend, and bade me tell the Reeve that I could join the castle harvest for a day when work began.

August 28th, Tuesday

I asked Oliver about fishing. He told me that all of the fish in the river belong to the castle – not just those in the stewponds fed by the moat's waters. Poachers steal many fish, he said, and they go to a different place each time so the Water-Keeper cannot catch them. He said the poachers grill their stolen fish on a single leek leaf, which holds it like a boat. I did not believe him, but when I asked Mark he swore it was true.

August 29th, Wednesday

The villagers hasten to cut their own corn, while the Reeve mutters and peers at the skies. For when Reeve feels the time is right, they must leave their harvesting and reap the castle corn instead. 'Tis called a "boon", which means my uncle commands the villagers to do this work for nothing – it is their ancient duty and they cannot refuse.

Cook and Brewess both curse, for all those who

harvest have a great thirst and hunger. By custom the castle must feed them and quench their thirst on a boon-day. But Mark says 'tis not all work, and there shall be some sport when the castle harvest is done. This is all that he will tell me, and he only smiles when I beg to know more.

September 3rd, Monday

The past four days being hot, the Reeve held off from the boon-work to let the corn dry further before it was cut. But today he would wait no longer, and straightway after Mass I hurried to the fields.

Already many people flocked around. The Reeve shouted at them to hasten, for he wanted near twenty acres cut today. The Reeve directs the harvest, just as he does most other business between castle and village.

I saw the poacher I had met by the river. He stepped up to me and said quietly: "Come lad. I did not mean to frighten thee t'other day." His voice was gentle, and I was

glad to know someone in such a large crowd of strangers. Seeing us talk, Reeve called out: "Ho, David! Thou and Toby are unlikely friends." There was much laughter at this, but David clapped me on the back and replied: "Aye, and he offers to bind my corn this day." So I set to work as a poacher's helper.

Everyone worked fast. The reapers bent double, grasping the stalks near the ground before cutting them. David watched me until he saw that I knew how to shake out the weeds and use the cornstalks themselves to tie up each bundle.

Folk paused from time to time to sharpen their sickles or mop their brows and drink from stone jars. For though the sky was dull the day was hot, and the work warmed them.

At noon, everyone rested and ate. Cook had set out mountains of bread, cheese and meat on wide boards laid across barrels. All who harvested could eat their fill of castle food, and wash it down with plentiful ale. The village folk drained in one day a barrel of ale so large it stood higher than my head.

The field in which we worked is 300 long paces across and as many wide, yet no more than forty men had cut all the corn by dusk.

When it was done, each reaper took as his right one sheaf of corn for each half-acre he had cut. David cursed as he lifted his. "This is miser's pay for such hard work," he said. I asked him what he meant.

"Boon-work is our duty, Toby lad," he replied. "None does it willingly. Each man has his own strips of land,

and to eat we must labour hard. Just when our crop is ready to be cut, so too is the castle's. But we gain nothing from the corn we cut today, for it feeds the castle folk." And with this he bade me goodnight.

September 4th, Tuesday

Today ended the boon-work. I slipped out to the fields as soon as lessons were over and, as Mark had said, there was a game.

As the sun was setting, the Reeve stood in the middle of the field and tossed high a sickle. With corn sheaves we marked a ring as wide as his throw was long. Then Reeve fetched a ewe and set her in the middle of the ring.

David bade me keep still and watch what happened next. "If sheep stays in ring until cock crows, the villagers keep her," he whispered. "But if she runs, 'twill be to yonder table," and he pointed up at the castle. None dared move save the Reeve. He coughed loudly, but it did not fright the ewe.

We had not long to wait, for in any village there are plenty of cocks, and before a moment was out one called and the village lads rushed forward to claim their prize.

September 5th, Wednesday

My venture in the cornfields has left me covered in the bites of harvest-mites, and no amount of scratching will relieve the itch.

October 10th, Wednesday

While crossing the Bailey this morn I heard a great commotion coming from beyond the castle walls. I rushed out through the gate and saw a crowd of villagers. In their midst was the Reeve, followed by David. Behind both walked the Water-Keeper. In one hand he carried a

small fish, and in the other he held a rope which was tied to David's wrists.

They walked with difficulty towards the castle gate, for the angry crowd slowed their pace. I saw many that I knew from the harvest.

Mark was there, too, so I asked him what had happened.

"Our Water-Keeper is all for locking David up, just for poaching a tiddler from the castle moat," he replied scornfully. "He lay in wait all night to catch him!"

At this I swear my mouth must have gaped, for I had thought David's ventures a secret only he and I shared. This made Mark laugh. "Didst thou not know? Fie, man, everyone in the village takes fish, and hare and pheasant!

Thus folk are angry, for they guess the Water-Keeper chose David on purpose, to warn others."

October 11th, Thursday

David is locked up beneath the gatehouse tower. Though he is a guest in the castle he is an unwelcome one, and would both starve and freeze if his daughter did not bring food and firewood to his cell. By crouching low I can peer in through a grating and look down into his cell. It is small and cramped, and so dark that I can scarce make out his face. It must be damp, too, for the moat is hard by, but he complains not.

October 22nd, Monday

Still David is kept within the cell. It seems he must stay there until the castle court meets next month. Small crimes my uncle judges, and chooses the punishment. But because David's crime is serious the King's judge must decide his fate, and he visits the castle only twice a year.

November 2nd, Friday

Now the weather is cold, and meat does not rot, the stockmen have begun the slaughtering. Pig and sheep are all slaughtered, save only those that are needed for breeding in the spring.

Isbel says: "Angels eat once a day, men twice, and animals thrice. Even a hayrick the size of the Keep would not feed all our livestock through the winter."

November 3rd, Saturday

I watched the pig-man kill a hog. First he fed her a bucket of acorns, and with his left hand stroked her back. Privily he held in his right hand a hammer. With this he did strike a blow to her head while her snout was in the bucket.

The blow felled her, and quick as a flash he cut her throat. Blood pumped into a bucket that stood ready, for nothing be wasted and blood makes a fine sausage.

I asked him how his left hand could be so kind, yet his right hand so cruel.

"Not cruel, lad," he replied. "Hogs live only for the day when they shall die and feed us. Yet not kind, either. We do stroke the hogs to calm them, for a happy hog makes tastier bacon!"

The meat must all be trimmed and cut and packed in barrels full of salt to last the winter. But not even salt will preserve the innards for long, so even the lowest servants can gorge themselves on brains and tripe and blood sausage, and for once all our bellies are full.

November 5th, Monday

David will be tried soon. I asked of Simon what would happen to him. "Yonder poacher?" he replied. "Let him rot in gaol for stealing our fish." But when I pressed him, he continued. "Poaching is a felony, so if the court finds him guilty, he shall be turned off."

At lessons later, I asked Mark what was meant by "turned off". He whispered back, "Why, hanged, you oaf! Executed." This so alarmed me that I dropped my tablet, cracking it into five pieces. Beaten once for each piece.

November 9th, Friday

The stockmen gave Humphrey some pigs' bladders. These we puffed up with air and sailed on the moat. At dinner we ate round, sweet puddings made of more such bladders, filled with pig fat and fruit, and then boiled.

November 22nd, Thursday

Tomorrow the Judge arrives to hear the cases that are to
be brought before the castle court. The Judge is the
King's official. It is his job to travel the countryside
hereabouts to ensure that lawbreakers are fairly tried.

The court is held in the Great Hall, and Mark has
explained to me how it will be (for he has watched
before). The Constable brings in each wrongdoer in turn,
and a jury, which is twelve men chosen from the village,
listens to the story of their crime. If the jurymen agree a
prisoner has done wrong, the Judge decides what the
punishment will be. If they think not, then the prisoner
is not guilty and is set free.

November 23rd, Friday

I crept into the Hall this forenoon to watch the court.
First the Water-Keeper recounted David's capture – he
was trapped with the fish in his hand, and two rabbits in
his bag. All were the property of my uncle. David hung

his head and my heart sank, for I feared no one would doubt his crime.

When David had spoken for himself, another from the village vouched that he was a good and godly man. But the Judge did not agree.

"Well, jurymen," saith the Judge. "You cannot doubt that this man is a poacher and a rogue. 'Tis clear he should hang this day." He let out a deep sigh, and asked: "Come men, what say you? Surely he is guilty?"

I held my breath while the jurors talked softly. Then the foreman (who is their leader) spoke: "Aye, sir, we all agree…"

The Judge turned to look at David. But then the foreman continued, "We all agree that he be not guilty as we see it."

At this the Reeve jumped to his feet and slammed his fist on the table. "Hell's teeth!" he shouted. "Shall we never stop these outrages?" The Constable scowled at David, and jerked his head to show that he could leave.

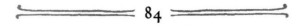

I jumped for joy to hear that David would be free, and rushed to tell Mark. He scoffed: "The Judge is an old fool, and the Reeve twice the idiot! The villagers would not send one of their own to the hanging tree, would they? Poacher he may be, but David will never suffer more than a spell in the dungeon."

December 7th, Friday

This morn my aunt told me that my father is coming! He is expected the day after the feast of Saint Stephen, and I am to return home with him to visit with my family. I cannot wait to see my mother and sisters again, though I shall sorely miss my friends here and hope they do not forget me while I am gone.

December 19th, Wednesday

Went to cut branches of holly and ivy to hang in the
Great Hall and elsewhere. Mistletoe, too, from the apple
trees that grow by the West Wall. At first Chaplain
would not let us bring mistletoe into the Chapel.
"A pagan custom," he called it. But my aunt ignored
him, saying: "Each year it is the same. Chaplain
dislikes mistletoe because it was held holy by those
who worshipped tree-gods. But their religion is older
than Christianity, so I see little harm in it."

December 25th, Christmas Day

There was dancing and jollity in the Chapel after Mass
this day, which again made Chaplain mutter about
pagans, but he would not (or could not) stop it. High and
low danced together, and those who came to wish us well
this day joined in the revelry too. Even Chaplain tapped
his foot when he forgot he should not. Then all the castle
folk gathered in the Hall – from the Constable to the

lowliest stable-lad. To each my aunt made a gift, and all thanked her kindly. I received an inkwell with a silver lid, and a tiny knife to cut goose quills into pens.

December 26th, Saint Stephen's Day

Dinner in the Hall today was a grand feast in honour of the saint. To celebrate Saint Stephen they do many things here of which we know nothing at home. Today, I learned, is a day for rewarding the castle horses. They are given a special feed and do no work at all, though not even Chaplain could explain why this was. Then I and the other pages went out to "hunt the wren", which is yet another old custom that is followed here. But though we took crumbs of bread and spent much time hiding in bushes, we could not capture so much as a feather to show for our pains. Had a grand snow battle, though, at which Mark and I were clearly the victors!

December 27th, Thursday

This day my father arrived, leading a second
horse for me. I had been looking out for
him from high up in the watchtower, and
as he neared I hastened out to greet him.

My father says we shall leave for
home early on the morrow, so I spent
what was left of the day in making my
farewells to my cousins and the many other friends that
I have made here. Mark and I looked for David in the village,
but though the fire in his house was still warm we found
him not, so Mark will tell him I am gone.

December 28th, Friday

Father woke me before dawn. We dressed and ate so quickly
I scarce had time to hug my aunt and uncle but we were
away. It is a long ride to Saltington, and my father desired to
use every moment of daylight for travel, though the moon
would light our way should we not reach home by nightfall.

When we had gone some way off, I heard the drumming of hoofs behind us. It was Simon hastening after us. "Ho Toby!" he hailed, and when we had halted gave me a long, slim parcel wrapped in cloth.

"Remember thine archery, Cousin," he said. "No bird is safe on the wing so long as thou practise at the butts." With this he slapped me on the back so hard I near fell in a dyke. We said one last goodbye, and he was gone again. Though I did not open my gift until we reached home, I guessed what was inside it.

As Simon left us I turned to look back at Strandborough. New-fallen snow dusted the tall towers, and on the highest I could see the watchman stamp his feet and blow on his hands to keep warm. 'Tis but a twelvemonth since I first saw that sight – yet somehow I fancied I returned home far more than a year grown.

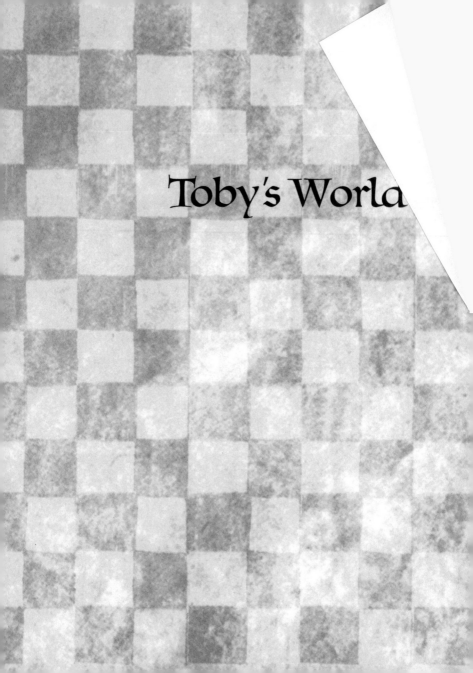

Toby's World

TOBY'S DIARY IS A STORY, but boys like Toby really did leave their families to work in castles as pages, and would have played the games his diary describes, and met people similar to those who appear in its pages. But although Toby wouldn't have known it, his uncle's castle was nearing the end of its useful life. Castles were built to withstand attack and in 1285, Europe was at peace. When wars began again, some fifty years later, new weapons and ways of fighting gradually made castles less important.

Toby's World

High and Low

As the Baron of Strandborough, Toby's uncle would have been part of the most powerful group of noblemen in his country – second only to a king or queen.

These noble lords controlled vast areas of land, and the castles that went with them. In return, they pledged their loyalty to the king and promised to fight in his wars and to bring an army of knights and foot soldiers with them. They also had to pay the king part of the wealth their lands brought them, as taxes.

Knights were noblemen who were also professional warriors. Each lord gave some of his lands and manor houses to his knights to use, to support themselves and their families. In return, the knights promised to fight for that lord and for the king.

All these noblemen had total control over the lands they were given, including the peasants – villeins and freemen – who lived and worked on their estates.

Villeins had to stay on the estate on which they were

Who Was Who in the 13th Century

king or queen

barons, earls, dukes, bishops and abbots

knights, noblewomen, priests and chaplains

freemen

and villeins

born, and could be punished for leaving it. They farmed plots of land and had to give their labour and part of their crops to the nobleman who owned the land.

Freemen had more rights. They could move to another estate, and laws limited how much labour they had to do on

their lord's land. Both villeins and freemen had to fight in their lord's army, though, and provide their own weapons.

Aside from the lords and their knights, the only other people of importance were high-ranking officials of the Church, such as bishops and the abbots of monasteries. These people might also be given land, but their only duty was to pray for the lord who gave it to them.

In western Europe, this way of organizing people according to their birth and the amount of land they controlled was called feudalism. However, by 1285 knights had begun to pay money to their lord instead of fighting in his army. And eventually, money payments replaced all of the feudal duties.

Younger Sons

In Toby's time, when a nobleman died his title and lands usually passed to his oldest son. And if he was wealthy enough, his other children might receive a "living", such as a manor house with some farmland.

As the younger son of a lord, someone like Toby's father might train as a knight but not be able to afford the expensive warhorse and armour that knights used in battle.

Instead, he could choose simply to live off his manor by farming his lands, or join the Church.

For noblewomen the only choices were to marry, to seek service with a wealthier noblewoman, or to become a nun.

A Page's Life

The sons of noblemen were often sent to live as pages in the household of a more important lord – usually by the time they were seven or eight years old. Here they were taught to hunt, to handle weapons, and to play games of skill, such as chess. They also learned how to be useful to their masters, and how to behave in noble society.

At the age of fifteen or sixteen a page became a squire. He acted as a personal servant to his master and rode into battle with him, often taking part in the fighting.

After about five years, a squire could become a knight. Any knight could award him this honour, although it was usually done by his master or by the king.

The Castle

For hundreds of years, warfare was used throughout Europe as a means of gaining power, wealth and land. And castles played a vital part in warfare.

A castle was a secure place from which to launch an attack, and a stronghold to retreat to after a defeat.

Castles were often built in a commanding position – to control a road or a river-crossing, or the land and people around them. And they provided safe homes, where their owners could live off the produce of their estates without fear of attack.

Like most European castles, a castle such as Strandborough would have changed over time.

New buildings and other structures would have been added to it as each generation of castle builders discovered ways of strengthening and improving its defences.

At the beginning of the

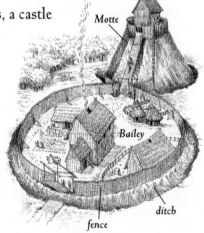

Motte

Bailey

ditch

fence

11th century, most European castles amounted to little more than a wooden tower, surrounded by a fence and perched on top of a mound of earth called a Motte. The owner, his family and his warrior-guards lived in the tower. Below the Motte, a second fence and a ditch enclosed a Bailey – an open space which could be used to protect local people and their livestock in times of war.

Strongholds of Stone

Motte-and-Bailey castles were quick and cheap to build, but castles of stone were stronger and provided better protection against attack by fire. Gradually, stone towers called Keeps began to replace the wood and earth fortresses, and a strong stone wall called a "curtain" wall was put around the Bailey.

Keeps varied, but most had living accommodation on upper floors, with storage rooms below. A raised doorway, reached by a staircase, allowed entrance to the Keep and was easier to defend than a door at ground level.

The weakest part of a castle wall was its gate, so this had to be especially strong. Often the gateway was part of a solidly built tower called the gatehouse.

By raising the drawbridge that spanned the ditch or moat

outside the walls, the gateway could be closed off with a solid wall of wood. Behind this a wooden grille, called a portcullis, could be lowered so that entry was difficult even when the drawbridge was down.

Next, defensive towers were added to the curtain wall. Because the towers stuck out from the wall, archers on the top could fire down on anyone at the wall's foot.

Battlements, too, were another cunning defence. These gap-toothed wall tops allowed archers to stand safely on the wall-walk behind the raised sections while firing through the gaps in-between.

By 1285, European castles had seen almost four hundred years of improvement. They had become immensely strong and almost impossible to defeat. In fact, the only reliable way to capture a castle was to surround it with a hostile army and try to starve the people inside into surrendering. This was known as putting a castle under siege.

Under Attack

By surrounding the castle, the attackers could stop food and other supplies from reaching it. Unless a supporting army could drive the attackers off, hunger would eventually force

Siege Weapons

1 MANGONEL: A large catapult powered by tightly twisted ropes, rather like a toy catapult uses a stretched rubber band.

2 BATTERING RAM: A heavy log swung from a wooden frame. It was used to smash through the gateway of a castle or to chip away at the walls. To protect the soldiers wielding it, the ram had a wooden roof built over it.

3 PAVISES: Large wooden shields protected the attacking archers from the defenders' arrows.

4 TREBUCHET: A giant catapult with a heavy weight at one end. Troops pulled the other end to the ground to load it with rock. When it was released, the weight crashed down and hurled the rock against the castle wall. Rocks weren't the only missiles that were thrown, though. Trebuchets catapulted beehives, rotting animal carcasses, even human heads.

5 SPRINGALD: A huge crossbow that hurled iron spears.

6 FIRE: Flaming arrows and pots filled with burning tar were fired at wooden doors and roofs.

7 SCALING LADDERS: These were used to try to climb over the walls.

8 SIEGE TOWER: A safer way to get inside was to use a wooden siege tower. A bridge could be lowered from the top of the tower to reach the battlements. Wet hides protected it from the defenders' fire, and earned it the nickname "the bear". Filling the moat with logs and rubble allowed the attackers to roll both the ram and the bear right up to the walls.

the castle to surrender. The attackers didn't just sit around and wait, though. They looked for cracks in the castle's defences – and if there weren't any they did their best to make some, mostly by using enormous weapons called siege engines.

The soldiers defending the castle did everything they could to hold out against the siege. Stocks of food and drink kept in the castle storerooms were carefully rationed. (Every castle had its own well inside the Bailey or the Keep, but even this could run dry, or the attackers might find a way to poison it.)

Protective wooden covers called hoardings were built over the battlements. These jutted out from the wall and gave the archers inside them a better view of the enemy. Also, holes in the hoarding floor allowed defenders to drop rocks on to anyone who tried to scale the walls.

Wooden roofs were built over tower tops, too, and covered with soaking-wet animal hides to resist fire.

But for every clever defence that could be found to strengthen a stronghold's weak points, there was always an equally clever method of attack.

Into Battle

A siege was a costly and time-consuming way to wage war. If a castle was well stocked, and its defenders determined not to give up, a siege could last for months or even years. And once the attackers had used up whatever crops or livestock they could find in the surrounding countryside, they had to bring in regular supplies of food from elsewhere or they too would starve.

A swifter way to victory was on the battlefield. But this had its problems too. Feudal knights only had to fight for their lord for a few weeks each year. And when their duty was done they could just pack up and go home.

By Toby's time, however, lords had begun to hire knights who would carry on fighting for as long as they were paid.

Battles often began with the enemy armies lined up opposite one another. Then the mounted knights charged, each aiming to knock their opponents from the saddle. Once on the ground, knights were hampered by the weight of their armour and were more easily killed or captured by the foot soldiers who followed the knights into battle.

Hand Weapons

Knights fought with swords and lances, but foot soldiers used many weapons, including swords, daggers and pole arms – long wooden poles fitted with axes, knives or spikes.

Pikes, for example, were like long spears. With the pole end held firmly against the ground and the point facing forwards, a row of soldiers with pikes made a deadly defence against charging knights.

Another favourite pole arm was the halberd. This had both a sharp spike and an axe blade, and could be used to hook or trip an enemy as well as stab and chop at him. Armed with a halberd, a foot soldier could hack at a knight's armour or at his horse, yet stay safely out of sword range.

From the 13th century on, archers too became increasingly important on the battlefield. They used both longbows and crossbows. Longbows required more skill (to shoot accurately, archers had to train from childhood), but an expert archer could fire six arrows a minute and hit a target 90 metres away. Some could fire twice

this many if their aim did not have to be accurate. A massed body of archers could make arrows fall like rain on their terrified enemy.

The crossbow had a power and range similar to a longbow, but drawing the bow (pulling back the string) and loading a bolt (a small arrow) was slow. Crossbow archers could aim and fire only one arrow a minute, but they needed very little training.

Armour

Just as castles needed strong walls, so soldiers needed strong clothing to protect them from enemy weapons. In Toby's day, the commonest form of body armour was chain mail.

Armourers made mail by linking tiny wire loops to form a kind of heavy metal fabric. A hauberk or coat of mail alone might contain 30,000 rings, each joined by hand.

A full suit of armour could weigh as much as 30 kilograms. It was stuffy and hot to wear, but because the weight was spread evenly around the knight's body he could wear it all day without becoming tired.

A Suit of Armour

A knight wore many layers of protective clothing. Getting dressed was a slow business and needed the help of a squire.

Undergarments protected the skin from bruises and rubbing:

1 DOUBLET: thick linen undershirt

2 AKETON: thickly padded undercoat

3 ARMING-CAP: padded headcover

4 LEATHER SHOES

Next the chain mail:

5 COIF: mail covering for head

6 HAUBERK: coat of mail

7 MAIL HOSE

Then came a layer of metal and hardened leather:

8 A COAT OF PLATES: like a leather jerkin lined with small overlapping steel scales

9 GAMBOISED CUISSES: quilted tubes (like legwarmers), pulled over the thighs

10 SCHYNBALD: shin guards of boiled leather

11 POLEYNS: metal kneepads

12 ESPAULERS: metal shoulder plates

And the final touches:

13 SURCOAT: long linen overcoat decorated with the knight's coat of arms

14 AILETTES: decorative shoulder pieces made of parchment or thin wood

15 BELT AND SWORD in a leather scabbard

16 GAUNTLETS: mail mittens or gloves

17 HELM with crest

18 WOODEN SHIELD

A suit of armour like this was worn for tournaments. In battle, knights wore a lighter helm and less-decorative armour.

The cost of a full suit of armour and a trained warhorse was very high and only the richest knights could afford them. Poorer knights often made do with bits of armour picked up from the battlefield or handed down to them from their fathers.

Foot soldiers wore far less armour than knights. They had to provide their own and few could afford to do this. Many had only a metal helmet to protect them, although a better equipped soldier might also wear a short-sleeved hauberk and a coif – a mail headcovering worn beneath the helmet.

Friend or Foe?

At the tournament or on the battlefield, colourful patterns called arms shone from shields and fluttered on flags. The use of arms began in the first half of the 12th century, as a way of helping knights to tell friend from foe on the battlefield when helmets hid their faces.

Each noble family had its own unique design and at first these were made up of simple shapes, such as stripes or crosses. The designs soon became more elaborate, though, including real or imaginary animals (such as the ravens on Toby's uncle's arms), or objects, like castles or swords.

The design was held within the shape of a shield, and when noble men and women married they joined the shields of their families together to make a new one. Usually they did this by painting the husband's arms on one half of the shield and his wife's on the other. And when their children married they divided the shield yet again, into quarters. So the arms of each generation became more and more complicated.

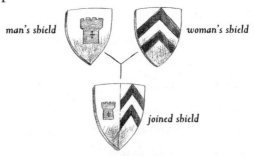

man's shield   woman's shield

joined shield

Keeping track of all these designs was the job of heralds and eventually this work, and the knowledge of how each design was constructed and what each part of it meant, became known as heraldry. Heralds had other tasks as well, though. They organized tournaments and other cere-monies, and acted as messengers on the battlefield, carrying instructions to troops.

Changing Times

As Toby was writing his diary, knowledge of a terrible new weapon was spreading across Europe. Over the centuries that followed, cannons would transform warfare – and in particular the role of castles.

Cannons were small and limited in range at first. But as they became more powerful, they were used with increasing success for destroying castle walls.

Thicker walls gave castles added protection, but by the 15th century cannons had become so effective that no wall could withstand their pounding.

Cannons, then, made castles useless, but other events had already begun their decline.

During the 14th century the plague known as the Black Death killed more than a third of Europe's people. Skilled workers were in short supply and those who had survived demanded better wages. This added to the already high cost of building a castle, so fewer and fewer new ones were constructed.

Feudalism was changing, too, and the kings and queens of Europe were helping to destroy it. They knew that a bold

lord who held many lands and castles could build up a strong army around him and could challenge their power – and some did. So they discouraged castle building, and banned lords from keeping private armies. In their place marched loyal knights who obeyed only royal commands.

By the 16th century, the age of the great fortress castle had come to an end. A hundred years later many castles were in ruins, and Toby's colourful world had vanished for ever.

Glossary
and Index

Glossary and Index

Page numbers that are <u>underlined</u> show where unusual words from castle times have already been explained – other unusual words are explained here. Words shown in *italics* have their own entries, with more information or pages to look up.

A

ACRE 73 About as much land as an ox could plough in a day. (2.5 acres = 1 hectare)

ALE 15, 32, 57, 63, 75 Alcohol brewed from barley.

ANVIL 48 An iron block on which metal is beaten into shape.

APPRENTICE 41 A trainee.

ARCHER 38, 101, 104, <u>106–107</u>

ARCHERY 35–39, 90, <u>106</u>

ARMOUR 40, 45, 51, 97, <u>107–109</u>

ARMOURER <u>41</u>, 107

ARMOURY 4–5, <u>40</u>, 48

ARMS (HERALDIC) 45, 108, <u>109–110</u>

ARMY 95, 97, 112

ARROW 36–39, 103, 106

B

BAILEY 4–5, 9, 51, 53, <u>100</u>

BANQUET 55, 58–64

BATTERING RAM <u>102</u>

BATTLE 105, 108

BATTLEMENTS <u>101</u>, 104

"BEAR" <u>103</u>

BILE 68 A fluid from the liver. Black bile was thought to be one of the four *humours*: melancholia.

BLACK DEATH 111 A terrible *plague* in the mid 14th century. Large swellings under the skin turned black and then burst.

BLADDER 82 The part of the body that holds urine.

BLAZON 45 To emblazon, or decorate.

BLOODLETTING 68 Opening a vein: the cure for most diseases in Toby's times.

BOAR 25

BOON 72

BOON-WORK 73–76

BOW (AND ARROW) 37–39, 106

BOWING 39, 49 Bending low to show respect or receive applause: a mark of *chivalry*.

BREAD 32–35, 63

BREAKING FAST 12, 19, 25, 51 Ending the nightly fast with a meal, breakfast.

BREWESS 32, 72

BUTLER 15, 62

BUTTS 4–5, 35, 36–39

C

CANNON 111

CASTLE DESIGN 99–101, 111

CELL 79

CELLARER 15

CHAIN MAIL 107

CHALLENGE 43 An invitation to a contest.

CHAPEL 4–5, 51, 86, 87

CHAPLAIN 19, 20, 86, 96

CHASE 28, 98 The hunt.

CHIVALRY 19 The *medieval* code of polite and honourable behaviour that *knights* were expected to follow.

CHRISOMER 41 Idiot.

CHRISTMAS 86

CHURCH 42, 97–98 The Roman Catholic Church, whose head is the Pope in Rome.

CLOTHING 41, 50

COAT OF ARMS 108 Originally a linen coat embroidered with a knight's heraldic *arms* and worn over his *armour*. Now used to describe the heraldic design itself.

COAT OF MAIL 51, _107_, 108
COCKATRICE _62_
COCK-CROW 51, 76
Daybreak, or any other time a
cockerel crows (which is often).
COLEE _52_
COMBATANT 49 A person
taking part in a combat, or fight.
CONSTABLE _17_, 35, 83
COOK 31–34, 72, 75
CORN 69, 71–76
COURT 79, 82, 83
CROSSBOW _107_
CUP-BEARER 63 The servant
whose job it was to fill people's
drinking cups at a _banquet_.
CURTAIN WALL _100_

D

DANCING 86, 87
DIZZARD 39 A fool or jester.
DOCTOR 65–68
DOGS 25–29
DRAWBRIDGE 4–5, 100–101
DUB 51 To make a _squire_ into

a _knight_ in a special ceremony.
DUNGEON 85
DYKE 90 A ditch.

E

EARL 55–56, 58, 62, 96 One
of the highest ranks of _nobility_
below the king.
EGYPTIACAL COTTON 41
Cotton from Egypt, and quite
costly in Toby's day.
EGYPTY DAY _50_
ESTATE 17, 56, 95–96
Property, including a castle or
manor house and its lands.
EWE 76 A female sheep.

F

FANFARE 63 A musical blast
on a _horn_ to announce an important person or event.
FARE 63 Food.
FARTHING 57 A silver coin
worth ¼ of an old penny.
FASHION 37 To make.

FEAST 52, 58–64, 88
FEIGN 49, 69 To fake.
FELONY 82 A serious crime.
FEUDALISM 95–<u>97</u>, 111
FINGER PILLORY <u>24</u> (Larger,
public pillories held criminals so
that passers-by could hurl insults
and rubbish at them.)
FIRE 103
FISH 42, 69, 70, 72, 78, 82
FISH DAY 42 One of the days
on which the *Church* forbad meat,
so people ate fish instead.
FLIGHT 37 The feathers at the
tail end of an *arrow*.
FOOD 31–35, 58–64, 101, 104
FOOT SOLDIER 95, 106, 109
FORENOON 21 Morning.
FOWL 62 Any bird suitable
for eating.
FREEMAN 96–97 Unlike a
villein, a freeman or freewoman
could choose where to live and
work. Their children were born
with the same rights.

FURNACE 40 A very hot fire.

G

GARB 41 Clothing.
GARDEROBE 53, 54 Originally
a room for storing clothes, but
also a polite term for a lavatory.
GATEHOUSE 4–5, 79, <u>100</u>
GONG-FARMER <u>54</u>
GREAT CHAMBER 4–5, <u>17</u>, 66
GREAT HALL 4–5, <u>9</u>, 10, 25,
52, 58, 83, 86
GUARD 35

H

HALBERD <u>106</u>
HALL See *Great Hall.*
HARVEST 71, 72–77
HEATHEN 50 Non-Christian.
HELM 40, 45, 48, 49, 51, 108
A type of helmet, encasing the
entire head.
HELMET 108, 109
HERALD 45, 48, 49, <u>110</u>
HERALDRY <u>110</u>

Romans, and still used for the *Church*, the law and scholarship in the *Middle Ages*.

⅏

N

P

PACE 44, 75 The distance between your footprints as you walk, about 76 cm. (2000 paces = 1 mile)

PAGAN 86 Non-Christian.

PAGE 7, 9–10, 12–13, 98

PALFREY 22–23, 52

PARCHMENT 31, 65 Beaten animal skin, used instead of paper for writing.

PAVISE 103

PENNANT 44 A small, pointed flag, displaying heraldic *arms*.

PENNY ALE 63 A weak and therefore cheap *ale*.

PHYSICIAN 65–68 A doctor.

PIG-MAN 80

PIKE 106 A *pole arm*.

PILLORY See *finger pillory*.

PLAGUE 111 A deadly and highly contagious disease, such as the *Black Death*.

PLAYERS 57 Entertainers: actors, musicians and acrobats.

POACHER 70, 72, 73, 74, 82, 84 A thief who hunts fish or game on someone else's property.

POLE ARM 106

PORTCULLIS 101

PREVAIL 44 To win.

PRIVILY 80 Secretly.

Q, R

QUILL 42, 88 A feather used as a pen until the 19th century.

RAM See *battering ram*.

REAP 72 To harvest a crop.

REAPER 74, 75

REEVE 17–18, 71–74, 76, 77

S

SAINT GEORGE'S DAY 40, 44 April 23rd: a holiday in memory of England's patron saint.

SAINT STEPHEN'S DAY 88 December 26th: a holiday in memory of the first Christian martyr.

SALLY PORT 30 A castle's back door, often a secret escape route.

SALT FISH 42 Fish covered in salt to stop it rotting.

SCALING LADDER 103

SCHOOLING 19, 20, 24

SCRIPTURES 19 The Bible.

SERGEANT-FARRIER 21, 22 The man in charge of the castle stables and horses.

SHEAF 75 A bundle of corn.

SHIELD 45, 52, 103, 108, 110

SICKLE 75, 76

SIEGE 101–104

SIEGE ENGINE 104

SIEGE TOWER 103

SMITH 41, 48 A blacksmith or iron-worker.

SOLAR See *Great Chamber*.

SPRINGALD 103

SPURS 45, 51 Spikes fixed to a rider's heels. Digging spurs into the horse's sides made it run faster. Some ceremonial spurs were gold-covered (gilded).

SQUIRE 8, 18–19, 49, 51, 59

STABLES 4–5, 21

STEWARD 15, 17 A *lord's* chief official, in charge of other servants.

STEWPOND 72 A large fish-pond.

STILTS 30

STOCKMAN 80 The man in charge of cattle and other livestock.

SUBTLETY 64

SUIT OF ARMOUR 107–109

SURFEIT 66 Excess.

SWORD 18, 52, 106, 108

T

TABLE MANNERS 56

TABLET See *wax tablet*.

TAX 18, 95 In Toby's day, any payment in money or goods that people had to make to *nobles*, or that nobles paid to the crown.

TOURNAMENT 40, 44–49, 108, 109, 110

TREBUCHET 103

TRENCHER 58, 63 A plate made of a slice of stale bread.

TUMBLER 57, 63 An acrobat.

Sources

Writers and illustrators owe a debt of gratitude to the authors and artists whose works inspire them. Richard Platt and Chris Riddell are especially grateful, because they searched in more than sixty books for details that would make the text and pictures of *Castle Diary* authentic. There isn't room here to list them all, but the following are among the more recently published books.

Bottomley, Frank: **Castle Explorer's Guide**

Bradbury, Jim: **The Medieval Archer**

Broughton, Bradford B.: **Dictionary of Medieval Knighthood and Chivalry**

Edge, David, & Paddock, John Miles: **Arms and Armour of the Medieval Knight**

Keen, Maurice: **English Society in the Later Middle Ages 1348–1500**

Koch, H.W.: **Medieval Warfare**

Leyser, Henrietta: **Medieval Women**

Miller, Edward, & Hatcher, John: **Medieval England: Rural Society and Economic Change, 1086–1348**

Muir, Richard: **Castles and Strongholds**

Nicolle, David: **The Hamlyn History of Medieval Life**

Norman, A.V.B., & Pottinger, Don: **English Weapons and Warfare 449–1660**

Pounds, N.J.G.: **The Medieval Castle in England and Wales**

Prestwich, Michael: **Armies and Warfare in the Middle Ages**

Saul, Nigel: **The Oxford Illustrated History of Medieval England**

Warner, Philip: **The Medieval Castle (Life in a Fortress in Peace and War)**

Woodcock, Thomas, & Robinson, John Martin: **The Oxford Guide to Heraldry**

Thanks are also due to the unknown artists who decorated **The Luttrell Psalter** (for Sir Geoffrey Luttrell of Lincolnshire in about 1330) with superb scenes of medieval life.

And to the staff of **Manorbier Castle** in Dyfed, Wales.

RICHARD PLATT has written over fifty books, and has a particular love for castles and all things medieval. He is also the author of the hugely popular *Pirate Diary*, Winner of the Kate Greenaway Medal and Smarties Book Prize Silver Award in the 6–8 category. Richard lives with his wife, a cat called Rabbit and three speckled hens called Dolly, Molly and Polly, in Kent.

CHRIS RIDDELL'S glorious illustrations spill off the pages of many wonderful children's books, including Hans Christian Andersen's *The Swan's Stories*, translated by Brian Alderson, which was shortlisted for the Kurt Maschler Award. Winner of the Kate Greenaway Medal for his illustrations in *Pirate Diary*, Chris was Highly Commended for the same award for its companion, *Castle Diary*. A brilliantly caustic cartoonist, Chris also works for *The Observer* and *The New Statesman*, and lives in Brighton with his family.